新文京開發出版股份有限公司

NEW
WCDP

新世紀・新視野・新文京 ─ 精選教科書・考試用書・專業參考書

Gerald Wayne and Faith Yeh

書中附免費下載 朗讀 **MP3**

QUANTUM
LEAP in English Learning

2nd Edition

TOEIC® & GEPT SKILLS BOOK
多益及全民英檢必勝指南

How to Use Quantum Leap in
English Learning

Quantum Leap in English Learning is versatile enough to be used in formal classroom settings, in informal gatherings among English students, and by individuals studying English on their own. Regardless of which of these means of study you're using, we urge you to invest in a reliable dictionary and a thesaurus.

Whenever possible, use English to learn English, just as you used your native language to learn your native language when you were younger. Some of your most useful tools will be reading, the dictionary, a thesaurus, and the Internet. When possible, let the English language speak for itself. Learning will be more rewarding and more enjoyable.

Depending on your level of English ability and your confidence, you may use any one of several study strategies or even a combination of strategies. *Quantum Leap in English Learning* features the kinds of exercises and questions that are found in the newest version of the TOEIC® test.

In this textbook, types of exercises are grouped together. Reading exercises are in one section, dialogues are in another, discussing what you see in pictures are in yet another, and so on. Feel free to begin with the sections that seem easiest or most interesting to you; or, if you wish, feel free to skip around, selecting from here and there as you would a buffet.

The lessons, as you would expect, are designed to be useful and interesting, but they are more than that. They are also designed to stimulate your imagination and your interest in the world outside your immediate surroundings, opening doors to cultures and lifestyles very different from your own. Make your English-learning an adventure in discovery and fun.

Once you've become familiar with the questions and answers in these exercises, create your own exercises for each lesson. Go to the Internet and seek further information on the vocabulary words and on people and things discussed in the lessons. You may plan an imaginary journey abroad and begin by checking actual car rentals on the Internet, or you may plan a vacation homestay in another land. We encourage you to use your imagination and make your own quantum leap into English language learning!

Contents

※掃描 QRcode，即可下載朗讀 MP3

朗讀MP3

朗讀MP3

Dialogues

Part 1 • **Out and About**

01
LESSON

Shopping

Ella: I'd sell my soul for a Gucci bag.

Amy: I'd like one, too.   Ella, they'll be on sale at 20% off.

Ella: Really?   Let's go this weekend.

Amy: We can't wait until the weekend.   The sale starts tomorrow.

Ella: But we have to work tomorrow.

Amy: Let's just take the day off tomorrow.

Ella: I don't know about that, Amy.   What if the boss finds out?   Our jobs will be on the line.

Dialogues

Reading

More Dialogues

Special Situations

Discussing Photos

Amy: He won't.   Don't worry.

Ella: Fine.   As long as I get my Gucci bag, I will be content.

Amy: We'd better go line up at five A.M..

Ella: What?   Why do we have to go so early?

Amy: We will need to fight for our bags.   There will be lots of people.

Copyright: Annto

True or False?

1. _____ Ella and Amy want to buy a Gucci bag.

2. _____ The sale on Gucci bags starts this weekend.

3. _____ The sale on Gucci bags starts in a week.

4. _____ Ella and Amy are waiting for the weekend.

5. _____ Ella and Amy have to work the next day.

6. _____ Ella and Amy are going on vacation tomorrow.

7. _____ The place that sells Gucci bags will be crowded.

8. _____ Ella and Amy plan to get up early tomorrow morning.

9. _____ Ella and Amy like to fight.

*   *   *

What about you?

Have you ever "skipped" school or work to do something fun that you don't usually do?   If so, tell about it.

Amy and Ella were talking about how much a famous brand (Gucci) meant to them.   What about you?   Do you get excited about famous brands, or do you think of yourself as more practical than that?   Give reasons for your answer.

Dialogues

Reading

More Dialogues

Special Situations

Discussing Photos

02
LESSON

Popular Movies: *Ghost Month Travelers*

Irene: Hi, Ellen!　How was your weekend?

Ellen: Great! My boyfriend and I went to see that new movie *Lorena*. You know—the one that's based on the novel *Ghost Month Travelers: A Supernatural Love Story*.

Irene: I wanted to go see it, but it sounds too scary for me.

Ellen: Oh, it has some scary parts, but it's mostly a love story.　Some Americans go on a vacation in Taiwan during Ghost Month; and it turns out they're being followed by the ghost of Lorena—a girl that one of the Americans had planned to marry eight years earlier. In all those years, Nelson—that was the American's name— had never married or even dated anyone else.

Irene: Oh, that's really sad. He must have really loved her.

Ellen: Later, they stay in a hotel that has hungry ghosts staying there.　The hungry ghosts try to take over Nelson's body, but Lorena saves his life.

Irene: Why would Lorena want to do that? If Nelson died, his spirit could be with Lorena again, forever.

Ellen: Lorena was willing to make the sacrifice for the man she loved, just as Nelson had given up eight years of possible happiness in memory of Lorena.

Irene: Oh, now it sounds really sad!　How could they ever be together again?

Ellen: The movie has a very happy ending—and it's very inspirational.

Irene: How can that be possible?

Ellen: I don't want to spoil the end of the movie for you.　You'll have to watch the movie for yourself.

Irene: Maybe I'll cheat a little by finding it in a book store and taking a quick look at the last chapter.

Ellen: Or you can go to the Internet and read the shorter version of the novel *Ghost Month Travelers: A Supernatural Love Story*.

Irene: Good idea.   I think I will.

Comprehension Questions:

1. By what means are Irene and Ellen communicating with each other?
   A. Over the telephone
   B. By email
   C. Face-to-face
   D. By Line.

2. What time of the week are Irene and Ellen having this conversation?
   A. Monday or Tuesday
   B. Wednesday
   C. Thursday or Friday
   D. Saturday or Sunday.

3. What did Ellen do during the weekend?
   A. She stayed at home
   B. She visited relatives
   C. She watched a movie
   D. She worked in her garden.

4. What was the name of the movie in this dialogue?
   A. *A Supernatural Love Story*
   B. *Ghost Month Travelers*
   C. *Ghost Month Travelers: A Supernatural Love Story*
   D. *Lorena.*

5. Where did the Americans in the movie go on vacation?
   A. America
   B. Japan
   C. Thailand
   D. Taiwan.

Dialogues

Reading

More Dialogues

Special Situations

Discussing Photos

6. What time of year did the Americans in the movie go on vacation?

    A. Spring

    B. Summer

    C. Fall

    D. Winter.

7. What was the scariest thing about the movie?

    A. Lorena

    B. Nelson

    C. Hungry ghosts

    D. The cost of the movie ticket.

8. What does Ellen like most about the movie?

    A. The beginning

    B. The middle

    C. The end

    D. None of it.

9. Why does Irene want to find the book *Ghost Month Travelers: A Supernatural Love Story*?

    A. To buy it for a friend

    B. To read it

    C. To see how the story turns out

    D. To see if the book is as good as the movie.

Discussion Questions:

How do you think the movie (or book) could have a happy ending?

Would you like to watch the movie or read the book?   Why or why not?

Tell about your favorite movie and what you liked about it.

What kind of books do you enjoy reading? Why?

Part 2 • Hobbies and pastimes

03
LESSON

Keeping Fit

Amy: Hey, Andy, why are you sweating all over your body?

Andy: I've just been practicing kung fu in the park.

Amy: Oh? How often do you practice?

Andy: About three times a week, if time permits.

Amy: Don't you get tired of all those workouts?

Andy: Not at all. I have patience. I really don't like the exercise it involves, but I do like the results. Amy, do you have any favorite exercises or sports?

Amy: Oh, no, I'm allergic to exercise. It makes me break into a sweat.

Andy: You really should get more exercise than you do. A sedentary lifestyle is bad for your health. Kung fu is a good aerobic exercise.

Amy: What's an aerobic exercise?

Andy: Aerobic exercises cause you to breathe more.   They're good for weight control.   You burn up more fat and usually don't get sore, as you would from anaerobic exercises.   Anaerobic exercises burn up more sugar, and they help to build muscles.

Amy: Well, I don't want to build up my muscles.   I think you're right about my needing aerobic exercises.   Maybe I can go with you next time.

Andy: That sounds great.   I'll be going the day after tomorrow.   Do you want me to give you a call to remind you?

Amy: Good idea.   I'll see you then.

Andy: Okay.   *Ciao!*

Inference Questions:

1. How often does Andy practice kung fu?
    A. Seldom
    B. Regularly
    C. Always
    D. Rarely.

2. How would you describe Andy's practice of kung fu?
    A. He gets a good workout
    B. He doesn't try very hard to get a good workout
    C. He's out of shape
    D. He likes to relax.

3. How does Amy feel about exercise?
    A. She likes to exercise
    B. She exercises regularly
    C. She dislikes exercise
    D. She wants to exercise.

4. What does Andy like most about practicing kung fu?
    A. Nothing
    B. The workout he gets
    C. It builds patience
    D. Staying physically healthy.

5. Which of the following exercises is aerobic?

   A. Walking fast for twenty minutes

   B. Lifting weights

   C. Rowing a boat

   D. Wrestling.

6. Which of the following activities is anaerobic?

   A. Bowling

   B. Tai Chi

   C. Lifting weights

   D. Dancing.

7. How often does Andy like to practice kung fu?

   A. Every two or three days

   B. Once a week

   C. Whenever he's not busy doing something else

   D. Every four days.

8. What does Amy plan to do?

   A. She has no plans

   B. Go with Andy to practice kung fu

   C. Go with Andy to watch him practice kung fu

   D. Watch a movie about kung fu.

Now read the entire dialogue from the beginning and discuss the answers with your teacher.

Now it's your turn!

Think of your own questions about this exercise and ask your friends and classmates. Be prepared to answer questions your friends or classmates ask you.

*   *   *

Photos in this lesson used under creative commons license:

http://upload.wikimedia.org/wikipedia/commons/1/13/Kung_Fu_Nuns_of_the_Drukpa_Order.jpg (Drukpa Publications Pvt. Ltd.)

Dialogues Reading More Dialogues Special Situations Discussing Photos

Dialogues   Reading   More Dialogues   Special Situations   Discussing Photos

04

LESSON

Caring for an Aquarium

*E*lla knows that Amy has an aquarium in her apartment.   Ella has recently bought an aquarium, so she is new to the hobby.   It seems, however, that both Ella and Amy are learning some hard lessons about caring for fish.

Ella: How are your new fish, Amy?

Amy: Some of them died a few days ago.

Ella: What happened?

Amy: My brother had bought new fish, and he didn't put them in a different fish tank, and it polluted the water.   Some of the fish got sick and died.

Ella: That's terrible!   I'll bet you were angry at him.

Amy: I was.   How are you getting along with your aquarium?

Ella: There's bad news from my place, too.   While I was washing my aquarium, my hands were slippery.

Amy: You broke it?

Ella: Yeah, I dropped it and it smashed into a thousand pieces.

Amy: What about your fish?   What happened to them?

Ella: Oh, I put them in the sink.   They look comfortable, but I think I should buy a new aquarium.   I think they would like it better than the sink.

Amy: Listen to yourself. How would you know if they're comfortable or happy? You're not a fish.

Ella: How would you know if I know if the fish are comfortable or happy? You're not me.

Amy: I know a couple of places you can get a new aquarium and I can get new fish. The two places are near each other, and, between the two of them they offer a wider selection than the store that used to be on Wen-lin Road in Shih-lin.

Ella: Where?

Amy: They're on Fu Hsing Road, a few blocks west of Shih Pai Road. If you like, we can go there this Saturday and I'll show you.

Inference questions:

1. Which of the following statements is most likely to be true?
   A. Amy bought a new fish tank.
   B. Amy's fish are cleaner than her brother's.
   C. Some of Amy's fish didn't die.
   D. Some of Amy's brother's fish are alive.

2. Which of the following statements is least likely to be true?
   A. Some of Amy's fish are still alive.
   B. Amy and her brother each have a fish tank.
   C. None of Amy's fish died yesterday.
   D. Amy's brother put his fish into Amy's fish tank.

3. Why did Ella mention that her hands were slippery?
   A. She had just washed her hands.
   B. Her slippery hands caused her to drop the aquarium.
   C. Her hands were not slippery before.
   D. The story doesn't indicate why she mentioned it.

4. What probably happened to Ella's fish?
   A. They smashed into a thousand pieces.
   B. They fell onto the floor and died.

C. They were in another container of water when the aquarium was smashed.

D. She scooped them up and put them in another container of water.

5. Where will Ella probably wash dishes until she buys a new aquarium?

A. In the sink.

B. In the new aquarium.

C. In a basin.

D. In the toilet.

6. How would you describe what Ella and Amy said about not being a fish?

A. They were joking.

B. They were arguing.

C. They were being philosophical.

D. They were trying to teach each other something.

7. Why does Amy think that the two fish stores will offer a wider selection of fish?

A. The stores are larger.

B. She knows the owner of each store.

C. The two stores are not likely to have exactly the same selections.

D. The same person owns both stores.

8. Why did Amy mention the store that used to be on Wen-lin Road in Shih-lin?

A. Ella probably used to buy her fish there.

B. Ella probably used to own the store.

C. The store in Shih-lin was closer.

D. She probably had no particular reason for saying it.

Now read the entire dialogue from the beginning and discuss the answers with your teacher.

*   *   *

Popular Novels: *The Fox Fairy of Kanifay Island*

LESSON

Alyssa: Hi, Sherri.   What's that you're reading?

Sherri: It's a novel called *The Fox Fairy of Kanifay Island*. I saw an abridged version of the novel for free on the Internet.   I thought it was so good that I ran out and bought the full-length novel.

Alyssa: What's a fox fairy?

Sherri: In this novel, a fox fairy is a girl that changes into a fox each night.

Alyssa: How does she use her powers?

Sherri: Well, I don't know if you'd call it a power.   Cindy—that's her name—is a Pacific island girl, and she can't tell anyone her secret. Cindy makes friends with a boy from America about the same time that a Hollywood actor is making a movie on the island.

Alyssa: Is the Hollywood actor the same age as the fox fairy?

Sherri: He's a young action movie hero a little older than Cindy.   He has a home away from Hollywood, and he has a helicopter.

Alyssa: Does anybody find out that Cindy is a fox fairy?

Sherri: Yes, everybody finds out, and she has to escape from the island.   The boy wants to help her to escape, but the army is watching the airport and the seashore to keep Cindy from getting away.

Alyssa: Wait a minute.   Cindy can't leave the island by plane because the army is watching the airport.   She can't go by boat because the army is watching the seashore.   How does Cindy escape from the island?

Sherri: I don't know.   I'm reading chapter 12 now.   I won't know until I get to chapter 13.

Alyssa: It sounds exciting!   If I can't find it in a book store, I'll look for it on the Internet.

Dialogues   Reading   More Dialogues   Special Situations   Discussing Photos

Comprehension Questions:

1. What do you think is the difference between an abridged version of a novel and a full-length novel?

    A. The abridged version tells the same story with fewer words

    B. The abridged version tells the same story with more words

    C. The abridged version tells a story that's different from the full-length version

    D. There's no difference.

2. Who is reading the novel?

    A. Alyssa

    B. Sherri

    C. Both Alyssa and Sherri

    D. Neither Alyssa nor Sherri.

3. Cindy (the fox fairy) makes friends with a boy from America.   When do Cindy and the boy talk to each other?

    A. Anly during the day

    B. Only during the night

    C. Both day and night

    D. The lesson doesn't say when they talk with each other.

4. Which city is closest to the fox fairy's island home?

    A. London, England

    B. Miami, Florida

    C. New York, U.S.A.

    D. Taipei, Taiwan.

5. Who is trying to catch the fox fairy?

    A. A Hollywood actor

    B. The army

    C. The police

    D. No one.

6. In the dialogue, the word *escape* is used three times; but other words are used to say the same thing.   Which of these words *cannot* be used in place of *escape*?

    A. Get away

    B. Go

C. Leave

D. Watch.

7. Why doesn't Sherri tell Alyssa how the story ends?

A. Sherri doesn't want to spoil the ending for Alyssa

B. Sherri is too busy to tell Alyssa

C. Sherri doesn't know how the story ends

D. Sherri didn't understand how the story ends.

8. What do you think Alyssa will do later?

A. Look for *The Fox Fairy of Kanifay Island* in a book store

B. Look for *The Fox Fairy of Kanifay Island* on the Internet

C. Either A or B

D. Neither A nor B.

Discussion Questions:

1. Why can't the fox fairy leave by car or bus?

2. We know that the fox fairy was not able to escape by plane or by boat.   How do you think she escaped from Kanifay Island? (The answer is in the story.)

3. Have you ever heard stories about fox fairies or about people turning into animals? Tell the class about it.

4. What do you think your life would be like if you turned into a fox every night?

5. What if you found out that one of your friends was a fox fairy? Would it change your friendship?   Explain your answer.

Dialogues

Reading

More Dialogues

Special Situations

Discussing Photos

Part 1 • The Environment

06
LESSON

Repurposing

Every environmental problem in the world is caused by only two things: 1.) pollution (trash, harmful things we breathe, and so forth) and 2.) using up things that can't be replaced, (oil, metals, and other things). Nobody is making any more oil or metals in the ground, and the world seems to be running out of fresh water.

Both kinds of problems I just mentioned come from only one thing: products; that is, the things we buy for our use.

We all know we should reduce our use of products by recycling and reusing things. We can also practice repurposing. Repurposing is finding uses for things other than the uses for which they were first made. To practice repurposing, we must learn to see things for their basic nature and not just for what we're told they are used.

For example, the purpose of a paper clip is to hold two or more sheets of paper together. If we see a paper clip for its basic nature, we see it as a small wire. We can use a small wire for many different things. If we have a paper clip, we probably don't have to go out and buy a roll of wire.

Likewise, we don't have to buy a box of sandwich bags because loaves of bread already come in bag-like wrappers. We can use and reuse an empty bread wrapper until the next loaf of bread is used up; then we can use and reuse the next bread wrapper as a sandwich bag. By doing this, we save money, get the benefit of a "bread bag," and protect the environment all at the same time.

Let's look at one more example. When a ballpoint pen runs out of ink, it's no longer a ballpoint pen, but its basic nature hasn't changed. It's still a hard plastic tube with a metal point at one end. It can be used for many things.

Whenever we repurpose something that has outlived its original use, we can get further benefits from it, both for ourselves and for the environment.

Remember the four *R's* and four *betters:* Reduce, Reuse, Repurpose, and Recycle. These habits are better for our lifestyles, better for our pocketbooks, better for our health, and better for the environment.

Discussion:

Look at the following list of things and ask yourself these two questions: a.) What is the basic nature of this thing, and b.) In what way(s) can I use it?

1. One broken shoestring

2. A paper clip

3. A ballpoint pen with no ink

4. A key ring with no keys (You already have a ring for your keys.)

5. An empty dog food bag

6. A Mylar® or foil candy wrapper

7. An empty soft drink bottle

8. A zip lock peanut bag with no more peanuts

9. One sock or stocking with a hole in it

10. An empty jelly jar

11. An empty plastic jar

12. A net bag that used to contain onions

13. A large plastic straw for pearl milk tea

14. Last year's calendar on a small card

15. A broken umbrella

16. A cover for a purse-size umbrella

17. A pair of jeans that no longer fit you

18. A seashell

19. A DVD disc cover

20. A DVD disc that no longer can be played.

Oh, by the way, did you know you can use a pocket calendar for more than one year? Except for leap years, a year is fifty-two weeks and one day long. If you want to know what day it was on May 1 of *last year*, just look at *this year's* calendar. If May 1 of *this year* is Wednesday, then May 1 of *last year* was Tuesday. Likewise, you can use last year's calendar this year by adding one day. For leap years, though, you sometimes have to add or subtract one more day. You can surprise your friends by telling them the day of the week five years ago or five years from now by subtracting or adding five or six days.

Dialogues

Reading

More Dialogues

Special Situations

Discussing Photos

07
LESSON

Helping the Environment while Helping Ourselves

As you learned in an earlier lesson, every environmental problem in the world comes from only one thing: products—the things that we buy for our use.

People tell us that we have to use pure products if we want to help the environment.   We have good reasons to buy products.   We need to eat and have a place to live.   We also want to enjoy life.   That doesn't mean, though, that using less products will cause us to have less happy lives.

You see, nobody buys a product because he wants that product. We buy products because we want to have benefits that we hope to get from that product.   For example, if you buy a cola, you'll drink it and no longer have the cola.   You'll be left with only a can; you never wanted the can.   You bought the cola because you wanted refreshment (to no longer be thirsty), flavor, and probably quick energy.

Colas and other types of sugared water don't give you as much benefit as you could be getting, and they're overpriced—mostly, you're paying for the can.   Instead of asking what brand of sugared water you should buy, it's better to ask two other questions:

1. What benefit(s) do I want?

2. What's the best way to get those benefits?

To get refreshment, flavor, and quick energy, you might take some fruit in a reusable plastic container and a bottle of water with you as you leave home in the morning.   You can always refill the bottle during the day. Here are four good results of doing this:

1. You get the same or more of the benefits you want.

2. It's much, much cheaper than sugared water. You can use the money you save for other benefits.

3. It's far, far healthier for you.

4. It's far, far better for the environment.

Discussion:

Let's look at some other environmentally harmful products, what benefits we want, and the best ways of getting the benefits we want.   Form groups of three or four students and discuss the questions, "What benefit(s) do I want," and "What's the best way to get those benefits?"

Air conditioners: You want comfort.   What are five things you can do to get the comfort you want?   How will these things help you in these four areas: 1.) better benefits, 2.) cheaper, 3.) healthier, and 4.) more environmentally friendly?

Ballpoint pens: You want something to help you to remember something, or to communicate with someone else, or to draw something. Name two or more things that will give you one or more of these benefits. How will these choices help you in some of the four areas mentioned above?

Games on Smart Phones: You want to improve your skill in making your eyes and hands work together, and you want to feel good about being able to do it. Name some better ways to improve your eye/hand coordination and feel good about it. (Note: Some are much healthier for you, and you don't have to buy anything.) How will these choices help you in all four of the areas mentioned above?

What are some other things you buy or want to buy?   (Examples: convenience store meals, portable music players, toys from department stores)   What benefits do people expect to get from those products? What is the best way of getting those benefits?   How will your choices help you in these four areas: 1.) better benefits, 2.) cheaper, 3.) healthier, and 4.) more environmentally friendly?

To learn more about how we can help the environment by helping ourselves, see **Benefits and Reality:**   https://benefitsrealityparadigmaclast.blogspot.tw/

Part 2 • Other Lands, Other Cultures

Confucius wrote, "Everyone is my superior in that I may learn from him."   What do you think?   Did he mean "everyone," or did he mean only people whose cultures are similar to his?   We know in our hearts that people of other cultures can learn from us, but can they teach us anything worth knowing?   In the following series, we'll see what we can learn from rainforest, desert, and island cultures.

08

LESSON

Traditional Knowledge

Can you imagine scientists, engineers, and medical researchers traveling halfway around the world to speak with rainforest natives?   Can you imagine marine biologists and weather experts asking primitive people to teach them things that they had not seen in any of their university textbooks?

It's true.   World-class experts commonly seek the knowledge and advice of people who may never have been to school, have never used a computer, and have never traveled more than a few kilometers from their villages.

Since 1991, one third of all new medicines have come from nature.   Many of these "new" medicines have been known to rainforest natives for thousands of years.

For that reason, pharmaceutical companies commonly send medical researchers to rainforest shamans to seek out their traditional knowledge.   When they learn of a natural remedy, they take the knowledge back to their companies and use their knowledge of chemistry and biology to mass produce medicines to sell on the open market.

Dialogues

Reading

More Dialogues

Special Situations

Discussing Photos

The Emberás of Panama and Colombia are one of many rainforest tribes whose knowledge is sought out by experts living in technologically advanced countries.

For the Emberás, however, this thirst for knowledge is a two-way street. Like many of the world's rainforest tribes, they have adopted modern ways that they have found useful to them, and they cling to traditional ways that seem more useful to them. They want the best of both worlds.

At Emberá Indian Village in Panama tourists can learn of Emberá culture, watch traditional crafts being made, participate in traditional dances, eat local foods, and learn something of Emberá herbal medicine.

Tourists are often eager to get temporary Emberá tattoos made from the juice of a local berry. Besides being a form of body art, these tattoos are a powerful mosquito repellant. Thus, average tourists and not only researchers can learn from the Emberás.

The Moken people of the Andaman Sea, around Thailand and Myanmar, though, are much more traditional, and they don't encourage tourism. Still, they're friendly and hospitable.

Many of the 3,000 Moken people live in small houseboats on the sea six months a year, so their lives depend on their knowledge of the weather and the sea. Weather experts, marine biologists, and many other scientists from around the world go to the Moken people to learn from them.

A few years ago, a major earthquake hit the area, caused a tsunami, and killed 172,000 people throughout the area of the Indian Ocean. Although the Moken people live in the areas most destroyed by the tsunami, not one Moken was killed. Because of the Moken people's traditional knowledge of the sea, they knew, several minutes before anyone else, that the tsunami was coming.

It's a bit humbling to see world-renowned business leaders, scientists, and other experts being educated and advised by men and women in sandals and bare feet. The proud are humbled, and the humble are respected.

Comprehension Questions:

1. Why do experts in this article go to rainforest villages?
   A. To teach them
   B. To laugh at them
   C. To learn from them
   D. To watch them dance.

2. From where do medical researchers get many of their ideas for new medicines?
   A. From traditional healers
   B. From television commercials
   C. By accident
   D. From their medical textbooks.

3. What does the article suggest about many new medicines?
   A. They have been known for thousands of years
   B. They come from plant sources
   C. They come from animal sources
   D. All of the above.

4. Why do experts try to learn about traditional healing practices?
   A. To try to understand the superstitions of other cultures
   B. Because they're sick and want to get well
   C. To stop them from doing it
   D. To make money from making the medicines themselves.

Dialogues

Reading

More Dialogues

Special Situations

Discussing Photos

5. How do the Emberás deal with their traditional ways in the modern world?

   A. They cling to their traditions and reject modernization

   B. They reject their traditions and accept modernization

   C. They try to accept the best of both

   D. The article doesn't say.

6. Which of the groups mentioned in this article make money from tourism?

   A. The Emberás

   B. The Moken

   C. Both

   D. Neither.

7. Why do Emberás wear temporary tattoos?

   A. For decoration

   B. As an insect repellant

   C. Neither A nor B

   D. Both A and B.

8. What valuable traditional knowledge causes experts from around the world to visit the Moken people?

   A. Traditional healing

   B. Weather forecasting

   C. Things that live in the sea

   D. Both B and C.

9. Why weren't any Moken killed by the tsunami a few years ago?

   A. They were the ones who had caused it

   B. They expected it

   C. They can run faster than other people

   D. The article doesn't say.

10. Of the groups mentioned in this article, which one is most likely to be known for their skill in making baskets?

   A. Emberá women

   B. Moken fishermen

   C. Traditional healers

   D. Marine biologists.

Discussion questions:

1. Would you like to live on a house boat?   Why or why not?

2. What handicrafts do you know how to do?

3. How good are you in forecasting whether it will rain today?

*   *   *

Photos in this lesson used under creative commons license:

http://commons.wikimedia.org/wiki/File:Mujeres_de_la_etnia_Ember%C3%A1.jpg (Ayaita)

http://en.wikipedia.org/wiki/File:Panama_Embera_0619.jpg

(Yves Picq http://veton.picq.fr)

http://commons.wikimedia.org/wiki/File:CasasWounaan.jpg?fastcci_from=15023 (Ayaita)

http://en.wikipedia.org/wiki/File:Moken_kids.jpg (Ronnakorn Potisuwan)

Dialogues

Reading

More Dialogues

Special Situations

Discussing Photos

Dialogues

Reading

More Dialogues

Special Situations

Discussing Photos

09
LESSON

Traditional Comfort

We all know that deserts are hot, but did you know that deserts are also cold? Yes, at night, even the hottest deserts can get very cold. So, how is it possible to get comfortable in a desert?

For thousands of years, people in all climates found ways to get fairly comfortable by working with nature instead of trying to fight against it. People in the arctic traditionally have lived in ice houses called igloos to keep out the wind and to keep in body heat.

Arabs are known for their loose-fitting, light-colored clothing that reflects sunlight. Because the clothing is loose fitting, it also casts shade on the body and allows air to circulate beneath the clothing and keep the body cooler. Desert nomads live in tents designed to work with nature rather than against it.

Much farther south, the desert of northern Namibia is known as one of the hottest places on Earth. That is where the Himba people live.

What do Himbas do to keep comfortable during the hot days and chilly nights? They also design their homes to work with nature instead of fighting against it.

The Himbas build dome-shaped homes made of sticks and clay. A Himba home is a bit like a cave, only it's built above the ground. Wherever you go in the world, earth-covered dwellings keep an almost constant temperature of around 60-65 degrees Fahrenheit (around 15.5-18 degrees Celsius).

A Himba home isn't really below ground, so the temperature isn't as constant as it would be in a cave. Still, the clay slowly absorbs heat during the day and slowly releases it during the night. Thus, some of the heat of the day remains in the clay during the night, and some of the cool of the night remains in the clay during the day.

Himbas don't have much cloth, so they can't wear Arab-style clothing to keep more comfortable when they're outside. What do they wear?

In addition to cowhide clothing, Himba girls and women cover their bodies with a type of reddish clay called ochre. The red ochre acts as a sunblock against the sun's rays. It's also a form of makeup to color the skin red; and, among Himbas, red skin is considered a sign of beauty.

As it is in technologically advanced cultures such as ours, Himba men don't wear makeup to look more beautiful. As the saying goes, "Black is beautiful."

Dialogues

Reading

More Dialogues

Special Situations

Discussing Photos

Comprehension Questions:

1. What is the temperature like in a desert?

    A. Hot

    B. Cold

    C. Neither

    D. Either, depending on the hour of the day.

2. What purpose do arctic igloos serve?

    A. They keep out the cold wind

    B. They keep in body heat

    C. Both

    D. Neither.

3. What kind of clothing do Arab nomads traditionally wear?

    A. Loose fitting and light colored

    B. Tents

    C. Red ochre

    D. Clay.

4. How would you describe northern Namibia?

    A. A jungle

    B. A desert

    C. Mountainous

    D. The story doesn't indicate.

5. What helps to keep Himbas comfortable in their homes?

    A. Air conditioners

    B. Campfires

    C. Ice

    D. Clay.

6. Who puts red clay on their skin?

    A. Himba girls and women

    B. Himba boys and men

    C. Both A and B

    D. Neither A nor B.

7. Why do they do this?

    A. It's war paint to frighten enemies

    B. To look more attractive

    C. For protection against sunburn

    D. Both B and C.

Discussion Questions:

What about you?

1. What do you do to keep comfortable on a hot day?   Here are some suggested answers for discussion:

    A. Turn on an air conditioner

    B. Turn on a fan

    C. Open a window

    D. Use a hand fan

    E. Wear loose, light-weight, comfortable clothing

    F. Drink more water.

2. What are some of the most environmentally responsible ways to keep comfortable on a hot day?

*   *   *

Photos in this lesson used under creative commons

http://en.wikipedia.org/wiki/File:Himba_Boy.jpg

(Thomas Schoch at http://www.retas.de/thomas/travel/namibia2008/index.html)

http://en.wikipedia.org/wiki/File:Namibie_Himba_0712a.jpg

(Yves Picq http://veton.picq.fr)

http://en.wikipedia.org/wiki/File:Namibie_Himba_0720a.jpg

(Yves Picq http://veton.picq.fr) (Remixed)

Dialogues

Reading

More Dialogues

Special Situations

Discussing Photos

Dialogues

Reading

More Dialogues

Special Situations

Discussing Photos

10
LESSON

Traditional Education

*E*ducation has been defined as "the means by which one generation transmits its values to the next generation." Education takes place all around us, and not just in the classroom. It includes schools, forms of entertainment, television commercials, and many other means by which we absorb values from other people.

How does traditional Pacific island education differ from education as it is known in global culture—that is, your culture and ours? For one thing, traditional Pacific island culture takes a different view of status symbols: things that we hope will cause others to respect us, and for us to have more respect for ourselves.

In global culture, our desire for status often comes from the size of a company's advertising budget. The more money a company spends on advertising, the more status people in our culture expect from wearing something that has that company's label on it. Many people are willing to spend twice as much for the label as they spend for the product.

In Pacific island cultures such as Yap, in western Micronesia, children are educated to seek respect in what they're able to do for themselves and for others in their communities. Although schools teach computer education as an important link to global culture, they also teach traditional skills such as the weaving of skirts and baskets, boat building, celestial navigation **[navigation by the stars]**, rope making, music, and dance.

From an early age, boys and girls learn to weave baskets from palm fronds, and they make the straps from rope they've made from plant fibers. They're attractive, useful, and last for years. Both men and women carry handbags.

Dialogues

Reading

More Dialogues

Special Situations

Discussing Photos

Every girl is expected to know how to weave her own skirts, and each skirt is unique. Wearing a Micronesian skirt with individual touches gives the girl or woman respect because it shows that she's a capable person. A Micronesian skirt can last a lifetime and be passed along to the next generation.

Boys and men often learn how to make traditional sailing canoes and to navigate by the stars. Since it takes months for several people to make one canoe, it belongs to all of them, and they can have fun together.

It takes several weeks to make a traditional woman's ceremonial dance costume. The "grass" skirts are actually made from hibiscus bark. The upper skirt, which makes the hips look wider, is made from strips of banana leaves. The belt is made of natural fibers and decorated with cowries—a kind of small seashell. The skirt is dyed with natural plant dyes. The leis they wear around their necks are usually made of hibiscus flowers and coconut leaves.

Yapese dances are both an art form and a means of storytelling. The men's marching dance originated as a means of warning enemies. The women's sitting dance started out as a means of dancing while making long trips by canoe. The exciting and graceful bamboo stick dance, performed by males and females from age six upward, was once a means of fighting. The women's standing dance has always been a way of welcoming visitors.

On many Pacific islands, including Yap, traditional islanders have found ways to enjoy the best of both global and traditional cultures.

Comprehension Questions:

1. What does the article say that we gain from education?

   A. Jobs

   B. Money

   C. Status

   D. Values.

2. Where does the article say that we get an education?

   A. School

   B. Movies

   C. Commercials

   D. All of these.

3. What is a status symbol?

   A. Something we have that causes others to respect us

   B. An advertisement

   C. Wealth

   D. None of these.

4. What kind of place is Yap?

   A. A country

   B. An ocean

   C. An island or group of islands

   D. The article doesn't indicate what Yap is.

5. What kind of climate do they have in Yap?

   A. Cold and dry

   B. Warm and humid

   C. Warm summers and cold winters

   D. The article doesn't indicate what kind of climate Yap has.

6. Who learns how to make a handbag from a palm frond?

   A. Boys and men in Yap

   B. Girls and women in Yap

   C. Everyone in Yap

   D. No one in Yap.

7. Which of the following statements is most likely to be true?

    A. Yapese women weave skirts to make money for their families

    B. Yapese husbands are too poor to buy their wives advertised skirts

    C. Weaving skirts is a popular hobby in Yap

    D. Yapese women are respected for being able to weave skirts.

8. What is a canoe?

    A. A kind of clothing

    B. A kind of boat

    C. A means of welcoming others

    D. Something to eat.

9. Which word best describes a Yapese ceremonial dance costume?

    A. Expensive

    B. Simple

    C. Comfortable

    D. Natural.

10. Which dance is likely to be the noisiest?

    A. Marching dance

    B. Sitting

    C. Bamboo stick dance

    D. Standing dance.

Discussion Questions:

1. What do you think of the remark that education is the means by which one generation transmits its values to the next?

2. Do you know how to make something by hand?   Tell us about it.

3. Of all the skills mentioned in this article, what would you most like to learn?   Why?

4. Which dance would you most like to watch?   Why?   Would you like to learn it? Why or why not?

*   *   *

Photos in this lesson used under creative commons license:

https://www.flickr.com/photos/dweekly/2849115699/sizes/o/in/photostream/

(David Weekly)

https://www.flickr.com/photos/dweekly/2849029219/sizes/o/in/photostream/

(David Weekly) (Remixed)

https://www.flickr.com/photos/dweekly/2849939176/sizes/o/in/photostream/

(David Weekly)

https://www.flickr.com/photos/dweekly/2849818176/sizes/o/in/photostream/

(David Weekly)

Dialogues

Reading

More Dialogues

Special Situations

Discussing Photos

Discussing Photos | Special Situations | More Dialogues | Reading | Dialogues

11 LESSON

Real Mermaids

For centuries, seafarers have claimed to have seen mermaids in the sea and by the shore. Are mermaids real?

Before we can answer that question, we have to ask, "What do we mean by *mermaid*?" If, by *mermaid*, we mean a creature that's half woman and half fish, then of course mermaids are not real. Science and experience teach us that only animals that are similar to each other can mate and produce offspring. Fish and humans are too different for this to be possible.

Rather than ask if the seafarers really saw half human, half fish creatures, it would be more reasonable to ask, "What could they have seen under the conditions that they saw it?"

People often say that the seafarers must have seen a manatee or a dugong—two very large animals that look like a cross between a seal and a garden slug.   Look at the picture at the top of the previous page and judge for yourself.   Do you have any trouble telling which one is the manatee and which is the mermaid?

Here's another suggestion:

The seafarers had to have seen something they had never seen before.   It had to have been something that, in some way, looked to them like women with fish-like characteristics.

Mermaid legends come mainly from Western Europe, especially from countries along the Atlantic coast of Europe.   Not one of these areas has a tradition of women working, diving, and swimming in and by the sea.   They must have been amazed at the sight of women swimming like fish and apparently living in the sea.

Apart from Western Europe, many places throughout the world have centuries-old traditions of "sea women," which is what the word *mermaid* means.

Even today, these mermaids can be seen in certain places along the coasts of Madagascar, South Africa, Brazil, and even some of the islands of Korea and Japan. Women more often become free divers (divers who dive without scuba equipment) because women can stand the cold better than men can, and they can hold their breaths for three minutes or longer.

Few of the Japanese divers—known as amas—are still young; and many are well into their eighties.   Although pearl and abalone farms have drastically cut into their trade, these women plan to carry on their 2,000-year-old tradition as long as conditions and their health will allow.

Comprehension Questions:

1. Where have seafarers claimed to have seen mermaids?

   A. By the sea

   B. In the sea

   C. Neither, since mermaids aren't real

   D. Both A and B.

2. What living things can mate and have offspring?

   A. Animals that are similar

   B. Any animals

   C. Plants and animals

   D. Only animals that are alike.

3. What is a manatee?

   A. It's a kind of dugong

   B. It's a kind of garden slug

   C. It's a kind of mermaid

   D. It's a kind of sea animal.

4. Which countries' seafarers claimed to have seen mermaids?

   A. Countries such as Madagascar and Japan

   B. Countries such as Spain and France

   C. Countries such as Brazil and South Africa

   D. Countries such as Korea and China.

5. Which of the following statements is false?

   A. Japanese amas can hold their breath for a long time

   B. Japanese amas often work in cold water

   C. Most Japanese amas are elderly

   D. Most Japanese amas are men.

   We began this series with a quote from Confucius. We'll end it with a quote from Plato:

   "Those who can see beyond the shadows and lies [phobias and prejudices] of their own culture will never be understood, let alone believed, by the masses."

*   *   *

Photos in this lesson are in the public domain.

12

Close Encounters with Other Cultures

Try to imagine a vacation like this:

You fly to another country, far, far away. As soon as you get there, you step into a **glass bubble** and travel to your hotel—a hotel very much like the hotels in your home country. You eat only foods that you eat in your home country. Each time you leave the hotel, you step into the glass bubble and travel about, seeing the culture but never letting it touch you in any way, and you never get to know the people of that culture.

Does that sound like a fun vacation? No? Except for knowing that you're in a glass bubble, that's really how most people vacation in other countries.

The opposite of a glass bubble vacation is the **immersive** vacation. That's the kind of vacation in which you really get to know the people and their culture, eating local foods, staying in local-style homes or hotels, and finding out what it's like to live in the culture.

Over 45 years ago, a scientist came up with the expression **close encounters** to describe experiences people say they had with UFO's or creatures from another planet. Let's use his ideas to describe *your* experiences with other cultures on our own planet.

Close encounters of the first kind: You're less than 150 meters from the local people. You can clearly see them and watch what they're doing. That's how most people spend their vacations in other countries.

Close encounters of the second kind: You can show your friends back home something that proves you saw the local people of that culture. It's usually a **souvenir** you've bought. Many tourists take pictures; often, the tourist may be seen in the picture.

Close encounters of the third kind: Actual contact with a local person. This usually means that the local person looked toward the tourist when the tourist took his or her picture. Especially daring tourists actually stand next to the local so that the local and the tourist may appear in the same picture. Tourists who are less brave may have his or her picture taken while the locals can be seen somewhere nearby. Very few tourists dare go beyond a close encounter of the third kind.

Reading Dialogues

More Dialogues

Special Situations

Discussing Photos

Close encounters of the fourth kind: A change in the way the tourist sees the local person. Instead of seeing the local as something to watch, the tourist sees the local as a person to know. The tourist and the local may have a conversation about something they have in common. When the tourist sees the local as more than just a performer or an object of curiosity, the tourist is beginning to step out of the glass bubble.

Close encounters of the fifth kind: The tourist and the local have conversations and act with each other in ways that have purpose, meaning, and cooperation. For example, instead of watching a festival, the tourist becomes part of the festival. The tourist may join in dances or parades or get involved in making crafts. For an hour or more, the tourist may even forget that he's a tourist.

Close encounters of the sixth and seventh kinds: Spending a long time living in another culture (sixth kind), or adopting the culture as your own (seventh kind). You can't have an encounter of the sixth or seventh kind during a two-week vacation.

In the first three kinds of encounters, the tourist is still in the glass bubble. In the fourth kind, the tourist is stepping outside the glass bubble. In the fifth kind, the tourist is beginning to step into the culture. In the sixth and seventh kinds, the tourist is truly in the culture.

Discussion:

What about you? (Either divide into groups for discussion or speak individually with the teacher.) Have you ever been to another country? Was it a vacation or some other type of trip abroad? Which kind of encounter did you experience there? What kind(s) of encounter(s) would you like to have with another culture? What if the other culture were very different from your own culture? What would you like to do there?

More Dialogues

Part 1 • Professional Situations

13
LESSON

> ### The New English Teacher (dialogue and reading)

Sarah: That woman seems to be trying to find a classroom, but she doesn't seem to know which room she needs to find. She may be late for her class.

Ben: I don't know. She may know which classroom is which, but she could be ambivalent as to which class she should take. It may be her first day at the language school, and she's trying to decide whether to go to the beginner's class, one of the intermediate classes, or the advanced class.

Sarah: I think I'll ask her if she needs help. Excuse me, Miss. May I help you find where you're going?

Woman: I'm looking for the novice English class. Can you help me?

Sarah: I'm sure I can, but I believe that your English is too advanced for the novice class. Would you like me to point the way to the upper intermediate or advanced class?

Woman: Thank you, but no. You see, I'm the teacher. My name is Eileen.

Questions for discussion:

1. Why did Ben and Sarah think that the woman needed help?

2. What did Ben think was the woman's problem?

3. What did Sarah think might be the woman's problem?

4. Who asked Eileen if she needed help?

5. When the woman, Eileen, told which room she was trying to find, what did Sarah think?

6. What actually was Eileen's problem?

7. What do you think **ambivalent** means?

8. How do you think the word **ambivalent** is different from a similar word, **ambiguous**? (Hint: Ben was **ambivalent** about asking Eileen if she needed help.)

(Later that day—a short reading)

Eileen has just finished teaching her first class at the language school, and she has a few minutes to relax.   On the bulletin board, she sees posters advertising opportunities for travel and education in faraway places.

To her left is a poster advertising educational and travel opportunities in Australia.   In one picture, two men and a woman are wearing swimsuits, bathing caps, and sunscreen.   No doubt they are posing for a picture representing a famous beach near Sydney, Australia.

To further make the connection between the poster and Australia, you see one of Sydney's best-known landmarks.   A kangaroo-crossing sign completes the picture.

Eileen is looking at a picture representing a snowy, scenic area.   It may be New Zealand, in the Southern Hemisphere; then again, it may be a ski resort area in some Rocky Mountain state such as Colorado.   The place in the poster also may be in Europe—such as the Swiss Alps, the Italian Alps, or Bavaria, in Germany.

Like most students and teachers in Taiwan, Eileen is curious about those places. Many English students and their teachers hope to travel to them someday. Maybe Eileen has her own plans for travel.

Now it's your turn!

If you had the opportunity, where would you like to travel? Why? What would you like to do there?

Dialogues

Reading

More Dialogues

Special Situations

Discussing Photos

14 Amy Rents a Car

*A*my and her family have just begun their vacation in the United States, and Amy wants to rent a car for a week.

Vocabulary
Coastal cities
Collision insurance
Compact
Economy-size
Family-size
Liability insurance
Luxury
Paperwork
Standard
Vehicle

Manager: Hello.   May I help you?

Amy: Yes, please.   I would like to rent a car.

Manager: Of course.   What kind of car would you like to rent?   We have **economy-size**, **compact**, **family-size**, and **luxury vehicles**.

Amy: Family-sized will be fine.

Manager: How many passengers do you expect?

Amy: Four, including me: my parents, my sister, and I.

Manager: For how long would you like to rent the car?

Amy: Well, what are the rates for six days?

Manager: That would be $26.99 a day, including **collision insurance**; but, if you rent it by the week, it will cost only $124.99 for the week.

Amy: Then I'll rent it for a week.

Manager: Do you expect to travel out of state?

Amy: No, sir, we plan to see the sights of Charleston, Myrtle Beach, and the Grand Strand.   We'll be staying in-state.

Manager: Would you like to have **liability insurance** or **standard collision insurance**?

Amy: Since I have a perfect driving record, I'll go with standard collision, please.

Manager: Very well.   (Aside): Peter, would you show her one of the **family-sized vehicles**?   (To Amy): The **paperwork** should be ready for you when you've made your selection.

Amy: Thank you very much.

Manager: Not at all.   While you're visiting the **coastal cities**, you might like to visit Hilton Head Island and Georgetown. All the cities you plan to visit are along or near Highway 17.

Amy: What can I find on Hilton Head Island and Georgetown?

Manager: Georgetown, like Charleston, is an elegant historical city; and Hilton Head is a luxurious beach island resort.

Amy: Okay, thanks.   I think we'll visit those places, too.

Dialogues
Reading
More Dialogues
Special Situations
Discussing Photos

Comprehension questions:

1. Why did Amy want to rent a car?

    A. To drive to the United States

    B. To visit her family

    C. To travel during her vacation

    D. She needed insurance.

2. What does the story indicate about the man at the car rental place?

    A. He was impatient

    B. Family-sized

    C. He was busy

    D. He was helpful.

3. Why did Amy choose a family-sized car?

    A. She was traveling with family members

    B. She had many things to carry

    C. She was traveling alone

    D. She was traveling in-state.

4. For how long did Amy want to rent the car?

    A. Two days

    B. Five days

    C. About a week

    D. Two weeks.

5. Where were the cities Amy wanted to visit?

    A. In the center of the state

    B. In the mountains

    C. Near the ocean

    D. The story doesn't say.

6. Why did the man in the car rental shop suggest that Amy visit Hilton Head Island and Georgetown?

    A. He had relatives there

    B. He thought they were better places to visit

    C. Those places have amusement parks

    D. Those places were in the same area that Amy was visiting.

Now it's your turn!

Let's do a little role playing.   Divide up into teams of two.   One of you will read Amy's part; the other will be the man in the car rental place.   After reading to one another, switch roles.   Then pretend that you are in the car rental place. What would you do differently in planning for your vacation in the United States?

Dialogues

Reading

More Dialogues

Special Situations

Discussing Photos

Part 2 • Food and Drink

15
LESSON

Lunch Plans

Amy: I've been filing orders all morning, and I'm ready for our lunch break.

Ella: Amy, where are we going to eat today?

Amy: I could go for some Italian food at Dimagio's Ristaurante. What about you?

Ella: I like it, too, but we went there the last time we ate out. Can we have Japanese food instead?

Amy: No problem.

Ella: Okay, Japanese food is second on my list of favorite foods.

Amy: Which restaurant sounds good to you?

Ella: I would recommend the Funikoshi Restaurant. They have a wide selection.

Amy: Do they have a sushi bar?

Dialogues

Reading

More Dialogues

Special Situations

Discussing Photos

Ella: Of course. Have you ever heard of a Japanese restaurant without sushi?

Amy: What about sake?

Ella: Yes, but are you sure you want to have it in the middle of the day?

Amy: Not really, but if I really like the place, I might get John to take me there on a date.

Ella: That's a relief. For a moment there, I was afraid you might have an alcohol problem.

Amy: You did look a little surprised when I asked you about sake. Say, it's almost noon. Let's go.

Circle the best response to the following remarks:

1. I've had a long, busy morning.

   A. Did you have a long, busy morning?

   B. So have I. I'm ready for a break.

   C. It's almost noon.

   D. What are your plans for this morning?

2. I didn't eat breakfast this morning.

   A. You must really be hungry.

   B. Breakfast is the most important meal of the day.

   C. What did you eat for breakfast?

   D. I have more work to do.

3. Did you hear that there was a new Italian restaurant a few blocks from here?

   A. No, I didn't.

   B. Yes, I did.

   C. I'd like to eat there sometime.

   D. I don't speak Italian.

4. I especially like Japanese food.

   A. Can you read a Japanese menu?

   B. I don't know.

   C. Why did you say that?

   D. There's a new Japanese restaurant near here.   Maybe we can eat there.

5. Would you like to eat at a Japanese restaurant or an Italian restaurant?

   A. Yes, I would.

   B. What sounds good to you?

   C. I like restaurants.

   D. I haven't eaten breakfast.

6. Have you decided where you would like to eat lunch?

   A. Yes, I have.

   B. I think I'd like to eat at the new Japanese restaurant.

   C. Do they serve sushi?

   D. I feel sleepy.

7. Can you tell me if they serve saki?

   A. They serve all kinds of Japanese drinks.

   B. Yes, I can.

   C. No, I can't.

   D. They serve Italian wine at the Italian restaurant.

8. Did you know that they're open from breakfast through dinner?

   A. I'm glad to hear that.   Maybe I can get John to take me there for dinner.

   B. I know it now that you've told me.

   C. Does that include both breakfast and dinner?

   D. Do they serve sushi?

9. Are you sure you don't want to eat Italian food today?

    A. Is there something else we can do with Italian food?

    B. Lasagna is an Italian food, isn't it?

    C. It's hard to decide.

    D. We can eat Italian food another time.

10. For a moment there, I was afraid you might have an alcohol problem.

    A. I was wondering why you were looking at me like that.

    B. No, I just like to drink saki in the middle of the day.

    C. When would you like to leave for lunch?

    D. On second thought, maybe we should eat at the Italian restaurant.

11. Say, it's almost twelve o'clock.

    A. Is that A.M. or P.M.?

    B. My watch stopped.

    C. It has been a long day.

    D. And I'm ready for lunch.

*   *   *

What about you?

What kind of foods do you like best? (For example: Italian, Chinese, Japanese, or English) What dishes do you like best? If classmates are not familiar with these dishes, describe them. Do you have a favorite restaurant? Tell about it.

16

Tea or Coffee

Many of the questions people ask are not direct questions. The questions may be suggested by other questions. For example, let's listen to the following dialogue between Ella and Amy:

Ella: Amy, Did you hear that there was a sale on Converse shoes downtown?

Amy: My old shoes are wearing out. This might be a good time to buy some new ones.

In the dialogue you just read, the question was phrased as a "Yes or No" question, but Ella was not expecting a "Yes or No" answer. She was asking the question to see if her friend was interested in going to the sale.

Some questions are called tag questions. Tag questions are questions placed at the end of the statement. People ask tag questions because they want the listener to agree with them. The listener may or may not agree. Let's read the following dialogue that contains a tag question:

Ella: These shoes are beautiful, aren't they?

Amy: Yes, they are, but I don't think they will fit me.

Most of the things people say in conversations are not really questions. People usually make statements about something and expect others to respond with their own remarks. For example:

Ella: I hear that the music was really loud.

Amy: Yes, I had to cover my ears.

Notice that Amy said, "Yes," as though she were agreeing to a "Yes or No" question. Then she made her own comment about the music.

At the end of the dialogue, you will respond either to Amy or to Ella. When Amy is speaking, choose the answers that you think Ella would give. When Ella is speaking, choose the answers that you think Amy would give. Now, let's go to our dialogue.

Dialogues Reading More Dialogues Special Situations Discussing Photos

Dialogue:

Amy and Ella are eating lunch in a local restaurant and Amy has noticed that Ella prefers tea to coffee.

Amy: Why are you ordering tea?   Coffee is fashionable nowadays.

Ella: It's got to be tea.   I love tea—green tea most of all.

Amy: Well, I guess you can't teach an old dog new tricks.

Ella: I'm not that much older than you are.

When I was your age, I liked coffee better.   I would drink four cups of coffee a day.

Amy: I'm fond of coffee, but that's overdoing it.

Ella: Recently, it has been discovered that drinking green tea has many health benefits.

Amy: I guess everyone has always been vaguely aware of that, but—well, I still don't know what tea is supposed to do for people.

Ella: For one thing, it helps to prevent cancer and tooth decay, and it has anti-oxidants that slow down the rate of aging.

Amy: *Anti-oxidants.*   We hear that word a lot these days.   What are anti-oxidants?

Ella: In some ways, the body is like a machine.   Putting white sugar into it can gum it up pretty much the same as putting white sugar into the gas tank of somebody's car (not that I've ever done that).

Amy: I'll bet.

Ella: The body can also get rusty, like a machine. *Rust* is another word for oxidation. Anti-oxidants fight that sort of thing.

Amy: Oh, that's good. You seem to know a lot about healthy foods.

Ella: Not really. To tell the truth, I have a better reason for liking green tea.

Amy: And what's that?

Ella: I've always had a sweet tooth, and I really like pastries. Drinking green tea helps to fight the tooth decay and oxidation that eating pastries might ordinarily cause.

Amy: Ha! Ha! You're not a health nut; you're just a nut!

This time, instead of testing what you remember about the dialogue, you'll have a chance to create responses to dialogue. Respond to the following remarks by circling the best response:

1. Ella, I see that you're ordering tea instead of coffee.
   A. I like tea much better than coffee.
   B. You have good eyesight.
   C. Thank you for noticing.
   D. It's green tea.

2. Ella, don't you like coffee?
   A. Yes, of course I don't.
   B. I like tea better than coffee.
   C. I do like coffee, but I like tea much better.
   D. The taste of coffee is too bitter.

Dialogues

Reading

More Dialogues

Special Situations

Discussing Photos

3. Amy, do you like coffee or tea?

   A. Yes.

   B. I like both.

   C. Coffee smells very pleasant.

   D. No, I like coffee.

4. Amy, when I was your age, I liked coffee better than tea.

   A. Yes, coffee is better than tea.

   B. How old are you?

   C. Coffee is more expensive.

   D. When did you start liking tea better?

5. Amy, your coffee smells pleasant.

   A. Why are you smelling my coffee?

   B. It smells pleasant, doesn't it?

   C. It also tastes pleasant.

   D. It's cappuccino.

6. Ella, drinking green tea has many benefits, doesn't it?

   A. Yes, it does.

   B. It has many health benefits.

   C. I really like the taste.

   D. I prefer it to red tea or black tea.

7. Ella, I don't know what anti-oxidants are.

   A. Drinking green tea is good for your health.

   B. They are something that slows down the rate of aging.

   C. I think I'll order another cup.

   D. I don't know what they are.

8. You've never put sugar into anyone's gas tank, have you?

   A. Not since I was in college.

   B. Yes, I haven't.

   C. No, I have.

   D. It messes up the car.

9. Amy, did you know that drinking green tea has many health benefits?

   A. Yes, I've heard.　So what?

   B. Really?

   C. Green tea looks a little strange.

   D. There's a fly on your cup.

10. Can you tell me some of the health benefits of drinking green tea?

    A. For one thing, it helps to prevent heart disease.

    B. Do they also have green tea?

    C. Yes, it does.

    D. I like green tea better than coffee.

11. They have a wide selection of teas at Walton's Health Food Store.

    A. Is that where you buy your tea?

    B. Do they also have green tea?

    C. Do they sell tea at Walton's Health Food Store?

    D. Do they also sell cigarettes?

12. Drinking green tea is good for your brain.

    A. That's good news.

    B. Is drinking green tea good for your brain?

    C. I prefer coffee.

    D. Duh.

13. You seem to eat a lot of candy.

    A. So do I.

    B. I like tea.

    C. Yes, I suppose I do.

    D. I like candy and tea.

14. I'm sure you've heard that drinking green tea helps to fight tooth decay.

    A. I'm glad to hear that.

    B. I like hearing it.

    C. Yes, drinking green tea is good for your hearing.

    D. Yes, I've heard that.

15. Ha!　Ha!　You're not a health nut; you're just a nut!

    A. You may be right. I've been called worse.

    B. Yes, nuts are healthy for you.

    C. So are you.

    D. I hear that Walton's has a wide selection of green teas.

*　　*　　*

17
LESSON

Ice Cream

Ella: Amy, in this magazine, here's an advertisement for ice cream.

Amy: But it's the middle of winter. You must really have a sweet tooth. Who'd want to eat ice cream now?

Ella: I would. It just so happens that this one is my favorite flavors of ice cream: Cookie Overload.

Amy: Cookie overload? What a funny name it is!

Ella: It has Oreo and chocolate cookies piled high above the ice cream. They have many funny names for their ice cream flavors.

Amy: That's interesting. Maybe we can go to eat there someday. I want to try the cookie ice cream with cherries. It looks delicious, and I think I'll be able to find another new one I'll like.

Ella: I think you'll find so many kinds of ice cream there, that you'll have a hard time making a choice.

Amy: Really? My mouth is watering already. Winter or not, I can hardly wait to try some.

Reading   Dialogues

More Dialogues

Special Situations

Discussing Photos

Ella:　Oh, how about tomorrow?

Amy:　Great!　This week's so tight that I need some sweets to increase my EQ—my energy quotient.

Ella:　Me, too.　Eating sweet foods always makes me feel better.

Pretend you're having a conversation with someone and tell how you would respond to what the person is saying.　Circle the best response to the remarks below:

1. This morning's paper has an advertisement for a new ice cream shop.

    A. Where is the shop located?

    B. Which newspaper is that?

    C. I didn't know you could read.

    D. Does it have a picture?

2. I wonder if they have butter pecan ice cream.

    A. Do you like butter pecan ice cream?

    B. Probably.　It's a popular flavor.

    C. Ice cream is ice cream.　What difference does it make?

    D. Don't drink carbonated drinks with ice cream.

3. Did you know they have 48 flavors of ice cream?

    A. Then they probably have some flavors I haven't tried yet.

    B. How do you know?

    C. Have you counted them?

    D. Yes, the ice cream does have a lot of flavor.

4. I've never heard of Cookie Overload.

    A. You haven't?

    B. Well, I have.

    C. It has a lot of cookies piled onto the ice cream.

    D. They sell Cookie Overload at the ice cream shop.

5. You must really like that flavor.

    A. What flavor?

    B. It's delicious.

    C. It doesn't cost very much.

    D. Yes, it's my favorite flavor.

6. It sounds delicious.

    A. What sound does ice cream make, anyway?

    B. Where can you buy it?

    C. It is delicious.　You should try it.

    D. I can hardly wait for the shop to open.

7. They have 48 different flavors, and every one of them is delicious.

    A. Let's go to McDonald's instead.

    B. I can hardly wait to try some of them.

    C. Don't forget to brush your teeth afterwards.

    D. How many different flavors do they have?

8. Isn't it a little too cold for eating ice cream?

    A. Ice cream is supposed to be cold.

    B. I like ice cream any time of year.

    C. Mind your own business.

    D. Isn't what a little too cold for eating ice cream?

9. I'm eager to try some flavors I haven't tried yet.

    A. I like Cookie Overload.

    B. How many flavors have you tried so far?

    C. Me, too.　I'm really looking forward to it.

    D. I hope the shop is clean.

Dialogues   Reading   More Dialogues   Special Situations   Discussing Photos

What about you?

1. Do you have a "sweet tooth"?

2. What's your favorite dessert or sweet snack?

3. Do you eat cold foods or drinks during the winter or hot foods or drinks during the summer?

4. What are they?

Riddle: What's the best thing to put into a pie to make it taste good?

Answer: Your teeth.

Dialogues

Reading

More Dialogues

Special Situations

Discussing Photos

18 Shih-lin Night Market

In this dialogue, you will learn to recognize other problems in comprehension. Some of the multiple choice answers don't match the question.

Selina: Vicky, do you have time for activities this evening?

Vicky: No, I need to go home and get something to eat.

Selina: I'm planning to go to the Shih-lin Night Market.   I haven't been there since it was renovated.

Vicky: On second thought, supper at the night market may be a good idea. Would it be all right if I go with you?

Selina: Sure. Let's go. I'm sure it has changed a bit. Can you show me around?

Vicky: Of course. They still have the famous Shih-lin sausages, little cakes, and big cakes.

Selina: They sound good.   Do they still have Shih-lin deep-fried chicken?

Vicky: Yes, they do.   I think it's delicious, but it's a little too spicy for me.

Selina: Then we can buy beverages to go with it.

Vicky: That's a good suggestion.   Pearl milk tea should go well with Shih-lin deep-fried chicken.

Selina: I think so, too.

Place a check mark in the blank beside the correct answer.

1. When was the last time Selina has been to the Shih-lin Night Market?
   A. _____ She hasn't been there because it was renovated.
   B. _____ She will go there when it is renovated.
   C. _____ She hasn't been there since it was renovated.
   D. _____ Vicky hasn't been there since it was renovated.

2. What does Vicky plan to do this evening?
   A. _____ She went home to get something to eat.
   B. _____ He plans to go home and get something to eat.
   C. _____ She's hungry.
   D. _____ Vicky plans to go home.

3. What does Selina plan to do this evening?
   A. _____ She hasn't been to the Shih-lin Night Market since it was renovated.
   B. _____ She plans to go to the Shih-lin Night Market.
   C. _____ She planned to go to the Shih-lin Night Market.
   D. _____ He plans to go to the Shih-lin Night Market.

4. What does Vicky think of having supper at the Shih-lin Night Market?
   A. _____ It sounds like a good idea.
   B. _____ She wants to know if she can go there with Selina.
   C. _____ Vicky told him that it might be a good idea.
   D. _____ She said it will be a good idea.

5. What does Selina say about the Shih-lin Night Market?
   A. _____ She thinks it has changed somewhat.
   B. _____ Selina thinks she has changed a bit.
   C. _____ Selina thinks it will change a bit.
   D. _____ Selina has offered to show Vicky around.

Dialogues   Reading   More Dialogues   Special Situations   Discussing Photos

6. What foods do they serve there?

A. _____ They still have Shih-lin sausages, little cakes, and big cakes.

B. _____ We still serve Shih-lin sausages, little cakes, and big cakes.

C. _____ The Shih-lin Night Market serves its famous sausages and cakes.

D. _____ The Shih-lin Night Market will serve Shih-lin sausages, big cakes, and little cakes.

7. What does Vicky think of the Shih-lin deep-fried chicken?

A. _____ The deep-fried chicken may be a little too spicy for him.

B. _____ He's a little too spicy for Vicky.

C. _____ It tastes good, although it is spicy.

D. _____ It was a little too spicy for her.

8. What does Selina advise?

A. _____ They can have drinks with the chicken.

B. _____ They bought beverages to go with the chicken.

C. _____ They can have beverages with her.

D. _____ Beverages go well with the spicy chicken.

9. What does Vicky suggest?

A. _____ He suggested that they buy pearl milk tea.

B. _____ Vicky said that pearl milk goes well with spicy chicken.

C. _____ She suggested pearl milk tea to go with the spicy chicken.

D. _____ She suggests pearl milk tea to go with the spicy chicken.

*   *   *

What about you?

Do you go to night markets?   Why or why not?   What do you like or dislike about them?   If and when you go, what do you most like to do there?

Photos in this lesson used under creative commons license:

http://commons.wikimedia.org/wiki/File:ShiLin.jpg (Kyle Mullaney May 2005)

Part 3 · Travel

19 LESSON

Making a Bucket List

Madison: Hi, Glynis.   What's that you're writing?

Glynis: I'm making up a bucket list.

Madison: With the winter break coming up, I thought you'd be planning a vacation.

Glynis: I am.   This is how I've decided to plan my vacation.

Madison: I don't understand.   You said you're making a bucket list—a list of things that you've always wanted to do that you've never done before. What does that have to do with planning a vacation?

Glynis: It's a different way to plan a vacation.   Most people take "branded" vacations; that is, they decide to go to a famous place and then try to figure out what they can do there.   With a bucket list vacation, you make a list of things you've always wanted to do; then you search the Internet to see how many of them you can do in just one place.

Madison: Oh, that sounds too complicated for me. I'd like to go to Paris.   I hear it's the world's most romantic city.

Glynis: Madison, tell me three things you've always wanted to do.

Madison: Oh, let's see. I'd like to go swimming with dolphins, learn to make a traditional basket, and ride a horse in a countryside area; but I don't suppose I could do any of those things in Paris, could I?

Glynis: No, you can't.   I got a few ideas from a video called "Planning Your Vacation (Branded Vacation or Bucket List?)" Now I'm writing a few ideas of my own.

Questions:

1. Who are Madison and Glynis?

   A. Businessmen

   B. Students

   C. Teachers

   D. Either B. or C.

2. When does this conversation take place?

   A. During first semester

   B. During second semester

   C. During the summer

   D. There's no way to tell.

3. What is a bucket list?

   A. A list of things you've never done before

   B. A list of things you'd like to do

   C. Both A. and B

   D. Neither A. nor B.

4. What is a branded vacation?

   A. A vacation you take because the place is famous for something

   B. Vacation in a place that has a famous logo

   C. Both A. and B

   D. Neither A. nor B.

5. What does the article say you can do in Paris?

   A. Swim with dolphins

   B. Learn to make a traditional basket

   C. Paris is the world's most romantic city

   D. None of the above.

6. Which of these did Glynis _**not**_ say she wanted to do?

   A. Learn a traditional dance

   B. Make a traditional basket

   C. Ride a horse

   D. Swim with dolphins.

7. After Glynis has made her bucket list, what will she do next?

    A. Ask her parents for money to go on vacation

    B. Go on vacation

    C. Search the Internet

    D. The article doesn't say what she'll do next.

8. From the three things Madison said she wanted to do, what might be a good place for her winter vacation?

    A. Europe

    B. Canada

    C. Japan

    D. Australia.

9. Where can you get ideas for making a bucket list?

    A. Internet blogs

    B. Internet videos

    C. Other Internet sites

    D. All of these.

Discussion:

List five things you'd like to do that you've never done before. Remember, you're listing five **_things_** you'd like to **_do_**, and they must be things you've never done before. Your list should not include places you'd like to go, things you'd like to see, or your life goals.

Discuss the things on your list with your classmates.

Where can you do most or all the things on your list?

20 Planning Your Vacation

Okay, you've already decided what you want to do on your vacation.   Then you've searched the Internet to find the best places to do those things.   Now what? How do you fit all those things into an **itinerary** (a schedule for places to go, times, and what you'll do) along with times to eat, places to stay, and how to get around?

You start by deciding on each part of your vacation.   Then you decide how you're going to fit the parts together.

Every vacation has five parts: 1.) **transportation** (how to get there, how to get around, and how to get back home), 2.) **food and drink**, 3.) **lodging** (where you'll sleep at night), 4.) **attractions** (things you'll go to see), and 5.) **events** (things you'll go to watch, or activities.)

Let's be clear on the difference between an attraction and an event.   The Leaning Tower of Pisa is an attraction; you don't do anything there, you just look at it, and it doesn't do anything unexpected.   A football game is an event because no one knows everything that will happen.   You may participate in some events, such as the Coney Island Mermaid Parade; but you don't participate in an attraction.

If the attractions or events are in different cities, you'll have to decide what kind of transportation you'll use.   If you drive from one place to another, search the Internet to find out how many minutes (or hours) it will take to get from one place to another, and figure that into your schedule.

Finally, your vacation should have a **theme**.   That is, what kind of vacation is it? Is it a close-to-nature vacation, a traditional culture vacation, a high culture (such as art or classical music) vacation, or something else? All five parts of the vacation should **fit** the theme of your vacation.

If, for example, you plan your vacation for enjoying traditional Italy, you should want to eat Italian food and sleep in an Italian-style home or hotel.   Chinese food would be a poor fit. If it's a close-to-nature vacation, you may go hiking, cook food over a campfire, and sleep in a tent. A five-star hotel would be a poor fit.

To plan the perfect vacation, then, you'll need to decide what you want to do, what kind of vacation it is, and where you can best enjoy the vacation, plan the five parts of the vacation, and fit them together into an itinerary.

Here's one more suggestion: Don't be disappointed if something doesn't go as you plan.   Unexpected events sometimes make the best vacations.

Discussion (give reasons for your answers):

1. Which of these is _not_ a kind of transportation?

   A. Bus

   B. Car

   C. Horse

   D .Itinerary.

2. Which of these is _not_ a kind of lodging?

   A. Bed

   B. Hotel

   C. A local person's home

   D. Tent.

3. What would you call a native dance?

   A. An attraction

   B. An event

   C. Either an attraction or an event, or both and attraction and an event

   D. Neither an attraction nor an event.

4. What would you call a Broadway (in New York City) performance?

   A. An attraction

   B. An event

   C. Either an attraction or an event, or both an attraction and an event

   D. Neither an attraction nor an event.

5. For a good fit, which of these would you most likely eat during a week-long nature hike?

   A. Hot dogs

   B. Pizza

   C. Spaghetti

   D. Steak.

6. For a good fit, which of these would you *not* eat during a visit to Rome, Italy?

   A. Hot dogs

   B. Pizza

   C. Spaghetti

   D. Steak.

7. For a good fit, where would you *not* sleep during a week-long nature hike?

   A. In a cabin

   B. In a cheap hotel

   C. In a sleeping bag on the ground

   D. In a tent.

8. What would you call an elephant ride?

   A. An attraction

   B. An event

   C. Transportation

   D. All three of these.

9. Which of these would you probably *not* do in a Pacific island village?

   A. Go swimming

   B. Eat fish

   C. Learn to make a basket from palm leaves

   D. Ride a camel.

Now it's *your* turn!

Choose a partner and plan a two-day, one-night vacation to somewhere. Talk about it in class.

21
LESSON

Vacation in Osaka and Tokyo

Ella: Anna, I haven't seen you for a few days.   Where have you been?

Anna: Oh, Ella, I went to Osaka, Japan.

Ella: Oh, really?   How was it?

Anna: Great!   Osaka's food is awesome!

Ella: I've been to Tokyo, but I've never been to Osaka.   Is there much difference between the two cities?

Anna: Actually, I didn't find much difference.   Both are large and busy cities.

Ella: I'm surprised.   I had thought of Osaka as being more in the countryside.

Anna: Not at all.   Since you like rural areas, I would go to Hokkaido if I were you.

Ella: Why?

Anna: Because they have a lot of delicious foods such as king crab; and they have much more snow in Hokkaido.

Ella: That's where I would like to go.

Anna: Then you'd better dress for cold weather.

Ella: Right!   Even Taiwan's weather is sometimes too cold for me.   I can't imagine how cold it will get in Osaka.

Anna: Ha, ha!   You mean Hokkaido.

Ella: Maybe we will go to Hokkaido next vacation.   Shall we?

Anna: Yes, but probably not anytime soon.   I'll need a rest from my last vacation.

Information questions:

1. Where did Ella go?
   A. _____ A few days
   B. _____ Osaka, Japan
   C. _____ Great!

2. How did she like the place she went?
   A. _____ She liked it very much.
   B. _____ Great!
   C. _____ The food was awesome.

3. What did she do there?
   A. _____ She ate Japanese food.
   B. _____ She took a hot spring bath.
   C. _____ The dialogue doesn't tell us.

4. Where did Ella go on her vacation?
   A. _____ She went to Tokyo.
   B. _____ Osaka is more rural.
   C. _____ The dialogue doesn't tell us.

5. What is Osaka like?
   A. _____ It's a crowded and busy city.
   B. _____ Osaka is more rural.
   C. _____ Anna didn't find much difference between Osaka and Tokyo.

6. Where did Anna suggest that Ella go?
   A. _____ Seafood
   B. _____ Hokkaido
   C. _____ Expensive

Dialogues

Reading

More Dialogues

Special Situations

Discussing Photos

Dialogues

Reading

More Dialogues

Special Situations

Discussing Photos

7. What kind of food did Anna say can be found in Hokkaido?

A. _____ Seafood

B. _____ Snow

C. _____ Tokyo

8. What else does Hokkaido have?

A. _____ Expensive

B. _____ Seafood

C. _____ Snow

9. What advice did Anna give Ella about going to Hokkaido?

A. _____ She suggested that Ella go to Hokkaido.

B. _____ She suggested that Ella dress for cold weather.

C. _____ She told her that Hokkaido was cold.

10. What did Ella say about Taiwan's weather?

A. _____ It's always cold.

B. _____ It sometimes gets too cold for her.

C. _____ It's colder than Osaka.

11. What did Anna suggest about her last vacation?

A. _____ It was tiring.

B. _____ It was cold.

C. _____ She went to Hokkaido.

12. What did Ella suggest about Osaka?

A. _____ It's in Tokyo.

B. _____ It's warmer than Osaka.

C. _____ It gets colder than Taiwan.

*   *   *

Now it's your turn!

Have you ever been to another country?   Where did you go?   What did you see and do while you were there?   (If you've never been to another country, describe an interesting place you've visited.)

22

European Vacation

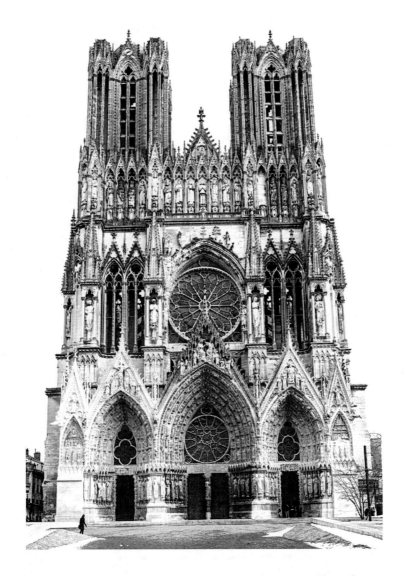

Amy: Ella, winter is coming soon.   Do you have any ideas?

Ella: I don't have any concrete ideas.   I may want to travel.

Amy: A foreign country?

Ella: I'll probably want to go to Europe.   I've heard it has a lot of beautiful scenery.

Amy: Yes, I've heard a great deal about the scenery in Europe, such as the French and Italian coasts.   Is there some place you especially want to go?

Ella: I especially want to go to Paris.   I hear that it's a cultural and romantic city.   I'd like to see the Cathedral of Notre Dame.   That is my dream.

Amy: Oh, me too, but it's too far away and too expensive.   I will go there when I have enough money.

Ella: I haven't decided myself.   After all, time and money are limited.

Amy: Ah! I have an idea where we can go. It has beautiful scenery, and it's not very expensive.

Ella: Really?   Where?

Amy: It's Taiwan.

Ella: Taiwan?

Amy: Yes, Taiwan.   There's Ilan, Hualien, and Taidong.   You can bask in a hot spring or dip in a cold spring, and it's much cheaper than the same things in foreign countries.

Ella: Oh, yes, that's right!   That sounds good.   Maybe I'll go to Hualien for this vacation.

Information questions:

1. When does this conversation take place?

    A. During the winter vacation.

    B. Just before the winter vacation.

    C. The dialogue doesn't tell us.

2. Where is Ella thinking about going?

    A. Winter is coming soon.

    B. Europe has a lot of beautiful scenery.

    C. She's considering Europe.

3. Where is Amy thinking about going?

    A. She may want to travel.

    B. She didn't say.

4. What does Amy like about Europe?

    A. Paris is romantic.

    B. She likes the scenery.

    C. It's too expensive.

5. Which parts of Europe does Amy like?

    A. She likes the seacoasts.

    B. Amy especially wants to go to Paris.

    C. It's a cultural and romantic city.

6. Why aren't Amy and Ella going to Europe this year?

    A. Paris is her dream.

    B. It's too expensive.

    C. She wants to go to Paris.

7. Why doesn't Ella know where she will go on vacation?

    A. She'll go to Taiwan.

    B. It has beautiful scenery and is not expensive.

    C. She doesn't have much time or money for a vacation.

8. Where does Amy suggest that they go on vacation?

    A. She hasn't decided.

    B. She said that Taiwan is a good place to vacation.

    C. Time and money are limited.

Dialogues

Reading

More Dialogues

Special Situations

Discussing Photos

9. What does Amy like about vacationing in Taiwan?

 A. Taiwan is beautiful, and vacationing in Taiwan doesn't cost very much.

 B. Amy suggested that they vacation in Taiwan.

 C. Ella hasn't decided where to vacation.

10. Where does Ella think she might vacation this year?

 A. She might vacation in Taiwan.

 B. She can dip in a hot or cold spring.

 C. It's much less expensive than going to Europe.

11. What kind of activity does Amy like in Eastern Taiwan?

 A. The scenery is beautiful and inexpensive.

 B. She likes hot or cold springs.

 C. You can do the same things in Europe.

12. Which three cities does Amy mention?

 A. Ilan, Hualien, and Taidong sound good.

 B. Maybe she'll go to Hualien this year.

 C. She mentions Hualien, Ilan, and Taidong.

*   *   *

What about you?

 What vacation spots do you like about the country in which you're now living? Try to mention some of the less famous places.

23
LESSON

Taiwan's Amusement Parks

Vicky: Selina, where are you going on your senior class trip?

Selina: I don't know. I've been to Leofoo Village and Window on China, and they're both good.

Vicky: Do you like any of the rides?

Selina: Oh, I like a lot of them. I don't know that I really have a favorite. I like the roller coaster, the free fall, and the pirate ship.

Vicky: Oh, that's a little too exciting for me.

Selina: At another amusement park, I once saw a little boy vomiting after riding on a roller coaster.

Vicky: That's terrible!

Selina: The next time I go, I'll probably ride the pirate ship. Would you like to go with me?

Dialogues   Reading   More Dialogues   Special Situations   Discussing Photos

Vicky:　No—thank you.　I don't dare.

Selina:　What do you like to do there?

Vicky:　Actually, I would like to ride the coffee cups and the bumper cars, but none of my friends want to go with me.

Selina:　No problem.　While you're riding the coffee cups, I can ride the pirate ship, and we'll meet after the rides are finished.　I bought some amusement park tickets for only a hundred NT dollars.　Do you want to go with me?

Vicky:　Sure.　I love the rides and foods at amusement parks.　One hundred NT seems a little cheap.　Where did you get tickets at that price?

Selina:　I bought them on line.

Vicky:　Are you sure that, at that price, they're not counterfeit?

Selina (looking at her tickets): I think you're right.　The name on the ticket is misspelled!

Vicky:　You've been had.

Information questions:

1. Where does Selina think she will go on her senior class trip?

    A. Japan

    B. An amusement park

    C. She will enjoy it

    D. She likes the rides.

2. What kind of rides does Selina like?

    A. She likes quiet rides

    B. She likes the roller coaster, the free fall, and the pirate ship

    C. She likes both Leofoo Village and Window on China

    D. She likes exciting rides.

3. How does Selina feel about Leofoo Village and Window on China?

    A. She likes both places

    B. She has already been to both places

    C. Vicky wants to go to both places

    D. She likes Leofoo Village but not Window on China.

4. How does Vicky feel about the rides that Selina enjoys?

   A. She vomited

   B. She feels that they are terrible

   C. She would be scared to ride them

   D. She likes amusement parks.

5. What happened to a little boy who rode on the roller coaster?

   A. He got sick

   B. He got scared

   C. He rode the roller coaster

   D. He'll never go back.

6. What did Vicky think was terrible?

   A. The little boy

   B. Selina

   C. The roller coaster

   D. That the little boy vomited.

7. What does Selina say she hopes to do at the amusement park?

   A. See the shows

   B. Ride the pirate ship with Vicky

   C. Eat refreshments

   D. Ride one of the rides.

8. Why won't Vicky ride the pirate ship?

   A. It's too scary for her

   B. She wants to ride the coffee cups and bumper cars

   C. She's afraid she'll vomit

   D. She doesn't want to ride with Selina.

9. Who wants to ride the coffee cups with Vicky?

   A. Selina

   B. The bumper cars

   C. The little boy

   D. None of the above.

Dialogues Reading More Dialogues Special Situations Discussing Photos

10. What does Selina suggest to Vicky?

   A. They will go to the amusement park with each other

   B. They will ride separate rides

   C. They will join each other after they have ridden their favorite rides

   D. All of the above.

11. Which things does Vicky enjoy at amusement parks?

   A. Eating the food and riding the rides

   B. The tickets are inexpensive

   C. She would be too scared to ride the pirate ship

   D. She likes popcorn.

12. How does Vicky feel about the cost of the tickets?

   A. She's surprised that Selina was able to get them

   B. She feels that it's strange that they were that inexpensive

   C. She's looking forward to the rides and amusement park food

   D. She's happy they could go to the amusement park together.

13. How did Selina get the tickets?

   A. They were cheap

   B. They were given to her by a friend

   C. She ordered them over the Internet

   D. The name on the ticket was misspelled.

14. Why did Vicky think the tickets might be counterfeit?

   A. They seemed too inexpensive to be real

   B. Selina had bought them on-line

   C. The name on the ticket was misspelled

   D. None of the above.

15. What was the next thing Selina noticed about the tickets?

   A. The name on the ticket was misspelled

   B. Selina had been cheated

   C. The tickets were very cheap

   D. All of the above.

*   *   *

Now it's your turn!

Do you like amusement parks?　Why or why not?　Among amusement parks you've visited, what's your favorite amusement park?　Why?

Dialogues

Reading

More Dialogues

Special Situations

Discussing Photos

Dialogues

Reading

More Dialogues

Special Situations

Discussing Photos

24 LESSON

Non-prose Reading

Many of the things you read are in incomplete sentences. A complete sentence has at least a subject and a verb, and it expresses a complete thought. In non-prose reading, the message you read may omit the subject, the verb, or even both. The complete thought is suggested rather than plainly stated.

In this lesson, you will be reading three examples: a public service advertisement, a lunch menu, and a want ad.

Now take a look at the three examples of non-prose reading and try to figure out what the incomplete sentences mean.

Neihu American School
presents

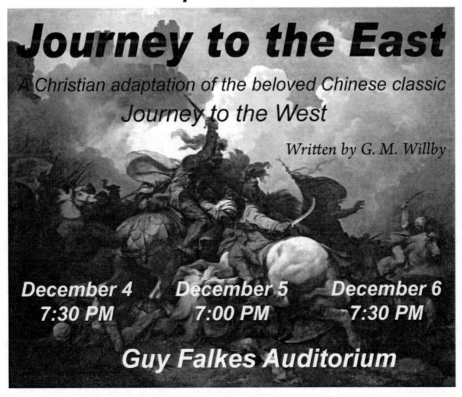

Questions:

In the blanks provided, select the correct answers.

1. What kind of event is announced?

   A. _____A movie   C. _____A play

   B. _____A speech   D. _____A radio program.

2. For how long will the event take place?

   A. _____One evening   C. _____Three evenings

   B. _____Two evenings   D. _____A week.

3. Where will the event be held?

   A. _____Guy Falkes Auditorium   C. _____Journey to the West

   B. _____Journey to the East   D. _____Neihu American School.

4. What is the name of the event?

   A. _____Guy Falkes Auditorium   C. _____Journey to the West

   B. _____Journey to the East   D. _____Neihu American School.

Now look at the menu below. It looks like any menu you'd see in your native language, except that it's in English.

The 76 Grill — Home of the Po' Boy Sandwich!

Main Dishes

Bacon, lettuce, and tomato sandwich	$4.75
Hamburger	$3.25
Cheeseburger	$3.75
Hot dog	$2.50
Chili dog	$2.75
Po' Boy sandwich	$5.75

Side Orders and Snacks

French fries	$1.50
Moon Pie	$1.25
Pork rinds	$1.50

Deserts

Chocolate cake	$1.25
Apple cobbler	$1.75
Blackberry pie	$1.50
Strawberry short cake	$1.50

Beverages

	Small	Large
RC Cola	$1.10	$1.25
Dr. Pepper	$1.10	$1.25
Ice Tea	$1.00	$1.20
Coffee	$1.00	$1.20

Lunch Menu

For this part of the lesson, let's try something a little different.

You'll need to find a partner for this one. One of you will be the waiter (or waitress). The other will be the customer. The waiter will take the customer's order. Select one item from each category. You may have to use a dictionary or the Internet to figure out some of the items on the menu, such as cobbler, blackberry, or short cake. Po' Boy (a colloquial form of "poor boy") sandwich is the local name for a type of sub sandwich.

Once you've placed your order, calculate your bill. Be sure to add 8% for sales tax. Then add 15% for a tip for the waiter (or waitress).

Now let's take a look at another example of non-prose reading—the want ad you see below.

Foreign Teacher Wanted

• **Must be a native English speaker**
• **Full-time or part-time employment**
• **Must be willing to relocate**
• **At least two years experience teaching English**

Hualien County

Please forward your resume to:

mskt@mail.hxcc.edu.tw
Cellphone:0920-246944

Walter
Telephone: (09)2109-6969

Questions:

1. What kind of teaching hours are being offered to the English teacher they hire?

2. What must the English teacher be willing to do in order to be accepted for the job?

3. What are the two qualifications must the teacher have?

4. Where is this teaching job?

5. What are the three ways a person could answer the advertisement?

*   *   *

Photos in this lesson used under creative commons license:

http://commons.wikimedia.org/wiki/File:Loutherbourg-Richard_Coeur_de_Lion_%C3%
A0_la_bataille_de_Saint-Jean_d%27Acre.jpg?fastcci_from=19493 (Ji-Elle) (Remixed)

25
LESSON

Advertisements

Mrs. McCoy's
Country Kitchen

Enjoy delicious, home-style cooking at Mrs. McCoy's Country Kitchen.

Mrs. McCoy's Country Kitchen is open daily from 6:00 in the morning until 10:00 at night. Our friendly staff cheerfully offers eat-in, take-out, and catering services.

Our menu offers a wide selection of mouth-wateringly tasty dishes in a very relaxing atmosphere. All the food at Mrs. McCoy's Country Kitchen is fresh and affordably priced. For a hearty meal, come to Mrs. McCoy's Country Kitchen.

As you can see, most of the copy for the commercial advertisement above is written in complete sentences. The words *Mrs. McCoy's Country Kitchen*, however, are not a complete sentence. What do those four words suggest? They suggest that Mrs. McCoy's Country Kitchen is the name of the restaurant. By <u>not</u> having *Mrs. McCoy's Country Kitchen* in a complete sentence, the advertisement is drawing special attention to the name of the restaurant.   Thus, people who see the ad are more likely to remember the name.

This correction was not made.   Please do so.   In an earlier reading lesson you saw advertisements and other published items that are written mainly in incomplete sentences.   In this lesson, however, we will discuss advertisements that are written mainly in complete sentences.

Dialogues Reading More Dialogues Special Situations Discussing Photos

Questions:

1. Which meal(s) can you eat at Mrs. McCoy's Country Kitchen?

   A. _____ Breakfast

   B. _____ Lunch

   C. _____ Supper

   D. _____ All of the above.

2. What kind of food is served at this restaurant?

   A. _____ Traditional American

   B. _____ Italian

   C. _____ Chinese

   D. _____ The advertisement doesn't say.

3. Which of the following does the advertisement not say about the food served there?

   A. _____ It tastes good

   B. _____ It's healthy for you

   C. _____ It's fresh

   D. _____ It's inexpensive.

4. Which of the following is not stated in the advertisement?

   A. _____ You can eat your meal in this restaurant

   B. _____ The restaurant will serve the meal somewhere else

   C. _____ The restaurant will allow you to take the meal home with you

   D. _____ The restaurant allows you to pick up your meal without having to leave your car.

Now it's your turn!

Using the above advertisement as your pattern, design an advertisement for your favorite restaurant. What do you think customers will like about the food at your favorite restaurant? What is convenient about your favorite restaurant? What else can you say in your advertisement that would cause people to want to eat there?

Dialogues   Reading   More Dialogues   Special Situations   Discussing Photos

An advertisement for a different kind of travel service

In the following advertisement, the first half of the copy is in complete sentences, while the second half consists entirely of incomplete sentences. Read this advertisement, then go to the next page to answer questions about it.

Adventure Vacations Travel Service

Imagine yourself vacationing among rainforest people in Panama or Indonesia, joining an adventure safari in the jungles of northern Thailand, participating in traditional South Pacific island culture, or witnessing the Umhlanga reed dance in Swaziland.

Adventure Vacations Travel Service offers vacations you will never forget–vacations away from glitzy, overpriced spots that are over-run with tourists. Adventure Vacations Travel Service offers getaway vacations steeped in traditional cultures and ecological discovery in natural, unspoiled settings while they yet remain unspoiled.

Call our toll-free number at 1-800-VENTURE

Enbera Village	Rainforest, Culture	Darien, Panama	3D4N	From NT$21,800
Northern Thailand	Rafting, Elephant Safari	Thailand	4D5N	From NT$12,300
Swaziland Tour	Umhlanga: Reed Dance	Swaziland	4D5N	From NT$23,400
Trobriand Village	Rainforest, Culture	Indonesia	3D4N	From NT$18,500
Yap Village	Diving, Culture	Yap, Micronesia	3D4N	From NT$13,800

Questions:

1. What activity would probably not be offered by this travel service?

   A. _____ Wearing native clothing

   B. _____ Dancing

   C. _____ Music

   D. _____ Native crafts.

2. Which food would you most likely find in the Yap village?

   A. _____ Fish

   B. _____ Beef

C. _____ Pork

D. _____ Insects.

3. Where would this travel service probably not take you for a vacation?

A. _____ Underwater

B. _____ Along a river

C. _____ A karaoke

D. _____ A warm country.

4. Which of these vacation destinations is most likely nearest the sea?

A. _____ Embera Village

B. _____ Northern Thailand

C. _____ Swaziland

D. _____ Yap Village.

5. How long is the vacation in northern Thailand?

A. _____ Less than four days

B. _____ Four days and nights

C. _____ Four days and five nights

D. _____ Five days or more.

6. Compared to vacations in Europe, Japan, or the United States, what can you say about an Adventure Travel Service vacation spot?

A. _____ It's crowded

B. _____ It's expensive

C. _____ It's educational

D. _____ It's air conditioned.

Now it's your turn!

If you were going on vacation in one of these spots, which would you choose, and why would you choose it?   Write down what you think you'd like to do for each day of the tour.

Plan your own adventure vacation and design an advertisement for it.

26
LESSON

How Do I Get There from Here?

Vocabulary and	other terms		
Across the street	Around the corner	Between	Behind
Block	Catty corner	Diagonally across the street	Facing (faces)
Next to	On the corner of _____ and _____	Turn left (right) at (on, onto)	Post Office

Asking for directions or giving directions is usually more than just naming streets and saying, "Turn left (or right)," and "You'll see it on your right (or left)."   It usually involves mentioning buildings or other places.   After all, buildings are much larger and easier to see than street signs.

Look at the image of the post office above.   The marks on the right side of the image—the ones that look like an equals (=) sign—show where the door to the post office is.   This can be important because doors don't always **face** the street.

For example, look at the bottom of the map on the facing page.   The Esso station **faces** the corner of Smith and Hill Streets.   The Esso station is **diagonally across the street** from Bendham's Yoga Studio.   The yoga studio is **across the street** from 76 Grill.   The 76 Grill is **next to** Yarborough's Auto Repair.   Yarborough's Auto Repair is **between** 76 Grill and Michelle's Driving School.   The driving practice area is **behind** Yarborough's Auto Repair.

Look once again at 76 Grill on the map.   Just above it, you will see where the Mims family lives.   See which direction the doors of these buildings **face**.   You wouldn't say that the Mims residence is **behind** 76 Grill because you don't actually go **behind** 76 Grill to get there.   From the front door of 76 Grill, the Mims residence is **around the corner from** 76 Grill.

A **block**, of course, is the distance from one street to the next street.   For example, Toby's Truck Stop is on Smith Street, one **block** from the Esso station.   You may also say that Toby's Truck Stop is about one **block** from the 76 Grill.

Dialogues

Reading

More Dialogues

Special Situations

Discussing Photos

A Map of the Downtown Area

(This map is not intended to represent an actual American town.)

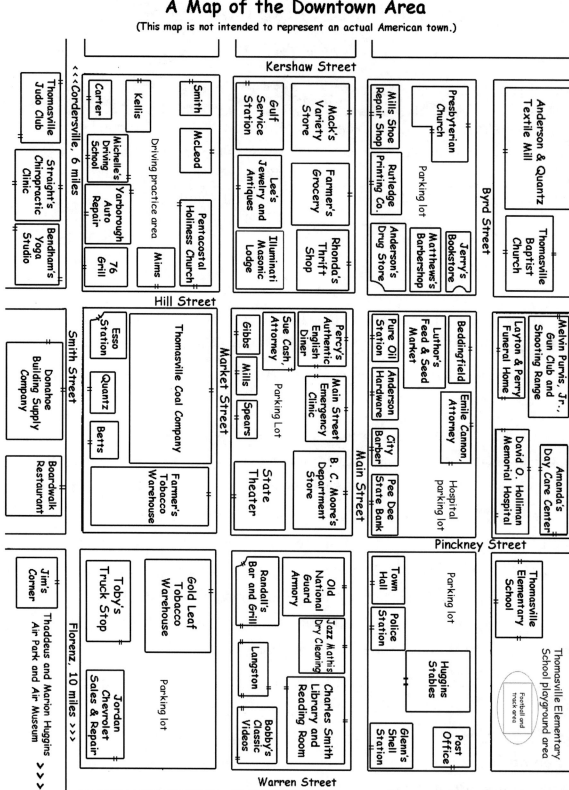

Sample Dialogue:

Serena (answering cell phone): Hello?

Sprite: This is Sprite.

Serena: Sprite, the movie is about to start.   I've been waiting for you.   Where are you?

Sprite: I'm sorry, but I'm lost.   I didn't think it was possible to get lost in a small town.

Serena: Well, what's the name of the place where you are?

Sprite: Mack's Variety Store, on Main Street, if that's any help.

Serena: As you leave the store, **facing** Main Street, **turn right**.   Go two **blocks** along Main Street and **turn right at** B. C. Moore's Department Store.   That will put you on Pinckney Street.   Go one **block** to Market Street.   The State Theater is **across the street from** Randall's Bar and Grill.   The front door of the theater is just **around the corner**, **facing** Market Street.

Sprite: I'm not on foot; I'm driving.   Where can I park?

Serena: You can park on Market Street **next to** the Gold Leaf Tobacco Warehouse.   The warehouse is **diagonally across the street from** the State Theater.

Sprite: Thanks.   I'll see you in a few minutes.

Now it's your turn!

Select a partner and create your own dialogue.

Dialogues

Reading

More Dialogues

Special Situations

Discussing Photos

Discussing Photos

27
LESSON

In the Office

In this series of lessons, you will practice discussing what you see in pictures. Look at each picture carefully.   Your teacher may discuss with you what some of the things in the picture are.

As you discuss the photographs with your teacher, feel free to make notes on the page you are discussing.

Let us begin.   Look at the first picture.

Accountant

Discussion Questions:

1. What is this woman doing?

2. Why is she smiling?

3. What is she wearing?

4. How would you compare her office space to that of the man in this lesson?

5. How does she look like the special assistant?

6. How would you describe her working space?

7. What are some of the things you see on her desk?

8. What else can you say about her?

Look at the following picture, where you see a woman sitting behind a desk.

Special Assistant

Discussion Questions:

1. What did the woman place in the vase on her desk?

2. Are they artificial or real?

3. What about the flowers in front of the vase?   Are they artificial or real?

4. Why do you think she is holding a pen while her picture is being taken?

5. Where is the woman's soft drink can?

6. Look at the pen in her hand, and the soft drink can.   Is she left or right handed?

7. A rolodex is in the upper right corner.   Do you know what a rolodex is?

8. How would you compare her to the other people in this lesson?

9. What else can you tell by looking at the picture?

Now take a look at the next picture, where you see a man sitting at an office desk and smiling at the camera.

Accounting Director

Discussion Questions:

1. What is this man doing?

2. Why do you think he is holding a large computer printout and a billing statement?

3. What do you think he will do with the red marker he is holding?

4. How can you know if the man is friendly?

5. Does he have a higher position than the others in the lesson?   Explain.

6. What is he wearing?

7. What else can you say about the man?

8. What else can you see in the picture?

Now look at the next picture, where you see a woman sitting in front of a computer screen.

Research Assistant

Discussion Questions:

1. What is this woman watching?

2. Where is her left hand?

3. Where is her right hand?

4. What is on the desk in front of her?

5. What else do you see on the desk?

6. What is on the shelf to her left?

7. How would you compare her to the woman in the second picture?

8. How would you compare her to the woman in the next picture?

9. What else can you tell from looking at this picture?

Now look at the next picture, where you see a woman standing in front of a desk.

Office Temp

Discussion Questions:

1. Where is this woman standing?

2. What is she doing?

3. What do you see on the desk on the left side of the picture?

4. What do you see on the desk on the right side of the picture?

5. What do you think she's holding in her hand?

6. What do you think is hanging from her shoulder strap?

7. How would you describe her?

8. How would you compare her to the office workers in the other photos?

9. What else can you tell from looking at this picture?

On your own:

Find a candid photo (a photo that the person or animals in the picture were not expecting to be taken) from the Internet or from somewhere else. What can you tell about the people, animals, or things in the picture?

28

LESSON

Around the Office

In this series of lessons, you will continue to practice discussing what you see in pictures. This time, the office workers are busy, but they're not behind desks. One works behind a counter, which is not the same thing.

Look at each picture carefully. Your teacher may discuss with you what some of the things in the picture are.

As you discuss the photographs with your teacher, feel free to make notes on the page you are discussing.

Let us begin. Look at the first picture.

Private Secretary

Questions:

1. What is this woman doing?

2. How would you describe her hair?

3. Where does she work?

4. What do you see on the counter next to her?

5. What else can you tell about the woman in the picture?

6. What else can you tell about other things you see in the picture?

Now go to the next picture, where you see a man standing in front of a large mainframe computer.

Computer Specialist

Questions:

1. What is this man doing?

2. Why do you think he is holding out his hands?

3. Why do you think he looks surprised?

4. How would you describe the shirt he is wearing?

5. Are the sleeves of his shirt buttoned or rolled up?

6. What else is he wearing?

7. What do you see behind the man?

8. What else do you notice in the picture?

Dialogues

Reading

More Dialogues

Special Situations

Discussing Photos

Now look at the next picture, where you see a woman and a man in an office.

Office Assistant

Questions:

1. Which of the people in this picture is standing?

2. Which one is sitting?

3. What do you see on the wall behind the woman?

4. Did the photographer mean to take a picture of the man or the woman or both?

5. Why do you believe this?

6. What is she wearing?

7. How old do you think the woman is, and why do you think this?

8. What color are the walls?

9. What else can you tell about the picture?

Now look at the next picture, where you see a woman standing in front of a billing notices printer.

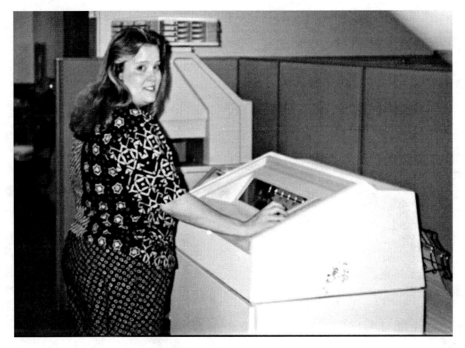

Billing Department

Questions:

1. What is this woman doing?

2. How would you describe her hair?

3. Compare her hair to the hair of the women in the other pictures in this lesson.

4. What can you tell about her age?

5. Of all the women in photos in this lesson, who is the oldest?

6. Who is the youngest?

7. Who is the slimmest?

8. Who is the heaviest?

9. How would you describe what the woman in this picture is wearing?

10. What else can you say about her?

11. What else do you see in the picture?

Dialogues

Reading

More Dialogues

Special Situations

Discussing Photos

Now take a look at the next picture, where you see a woman sitting behind a counter.

Receptionist

Discussion Questions:

1. Where is this woman?

2. What is she doing?

3. Where is she looking?

4. About how old is she?

5. How would you describe her hair?

6. What else can you say about her?

On your own:

Find a candid photo (a photo that the person or animals in the picture was not expecting to be taken) from the Internet or from somewhere else. What can you tell about the people, animals, or things in the picture?

29
LESSON

Around the City

In this lesson, we'll look at other things people do for a living. The people in the pictures include office staff, school teachers, a Chinese medicine shop owner, a policeman, and a traditional Chinese hair remover.

Let's look at the first picture:

Kindergarten Teachers

Discussion Questions:

1. What are these children doing?

2. Why are they doing this?

3. How many adults do you see in this picture?

4. Which woman is more casually dressed?

5. What is the woman in the right side of this picture wearing?

6. What is the woman in the left side of the picture wearing?

7. How would you compare their hair?

8. Which of these women do you think is the children's usual teacher?   Why?

9. What else can you tell by looking at the picture?

Dialogues   Reading   More Dialogues   Special Situations   Discussing Photos

Let's take a very close look at the next picture, where you see two men standing behind a counter.

Chinese Pharmacists

Discussion Questions:

1. Where do these men work?

2. Which man is the boss, the one in the background or the one in the foreground?

3. What is the man in the foreground doing?

4. What is he holding in his hand?

5. Who is the man in the background?

6. What is the man in the background doing?

7. Which man is holding a dish of traditional Chinese medicinal herbs?

8. What do you see behind them?

9. In the far right, can you see someone else?   What do you think he's doing?

10. What else can you tell from this picture?

The next picture was taken on a sidewalk. Let's take a look and discuss what the women are doing.

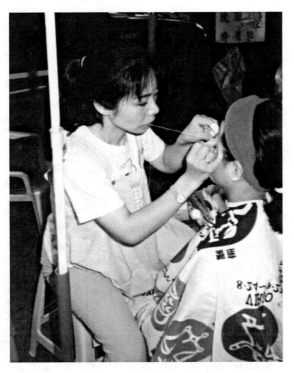

Traditional Chinese Hair Removal Specialist

Discussion Questions:

1. What is the woman in this picture holding in her hand?

2. Where is the other end of the string?

3. Why is she doing this?

4. Where do you think this picture was taken?

5. Is she sitting on a stool or some other kind of seat?   How can you tell?

6. What does it look as though she is wearing?

7. Why do you think there's a pole next to where the woman is sitting?

8. How would you compare the two women in the picture?

9. What else can you tell from looking at the picture?

Dialogues

Reading

More Dialogues

Special Situations

Discussing Photos

The next picture was taken in a cram school classroom.   Let's take a look and discuss what the teacher and students are doing.

Cram School Teacher

Discussion Questions:

1. Which person in this picture is the teacher?   How do you know?

2. What do you think he teaches?   Why do you believe this?

3. Why do you think the teacher has his hand to his mouth?

4. What are the ages of the students?

5. What are most of the students doing?

6. What is the student nearest the teacher doing?

7. Is the student in the white shirt opening or closing the plastic bottle?*

8. How many students are in the classroom?

9. What else can you tell by looking at this picture?

   *Is she opening the bottle or closing it?   Hold a plastic bottle.   As you remove the cap, notice where your elbow is pointing.   Now close the bottle and notice your elbow.   Is she opening it or closing it?   You decide.

Now let's look at the next picture and see what we can learn about what's happening and what the person is doing.

Policeman

Discussion Questions:

1. Who is this man?

2. What is he doing?

3. Why is he taking pictures?

4. What do you think happened in the accident?

5. Where do you think the accident happened?

6. Were the other two scooters in the accident?   Why do you believe this?

7. What else can you tell from this picture?

On your own:

Improve your detective skills.   Find other candid (not posed) pictures and see what you can tell about them.

Dialogues

Reading

More Dialogues

Special Situations

Discussing Photos

MEMO

MEMO

MEMO

MEMO

國家圖書館出版品預行編目資料

Quantum leap in English learning / Gerald Wayne, Faith Yeh 編著.－ 二版. －新北市:新文京開發, 2019.02
面 ； 公分

ISBN 978-986-430-479-0（平裝）

1. 英語 2. 讀本

805.18   108000980

Quantum Leap in English Learning
（第二版）

（書號：E409e2）

編 著 者	Gerald Wayne Faith Yeh
出 版 者	新文京開發出版股份有限公司
地 址	新北市中和區中山路二段 362 號 9 樓
電 話	(02) 2244-8188（代表號）
F A X	(02) 2244-8189
郵 撥	1958730-2
初 版	西元 2014 年 08 月 15 日
二 版	西元 2019 年 02 月 01 日
二版二刷	西元 2023 年 08 月 20 日

法律顧問：蕭雄淋律師
ISBN 978-986-430-479-0

New Wun Ching Developmental Publishing Co., Ltd.

New Age · New Choice · The Best Selected Educational Publications—NEW WCDP

新文京開發出版股份有限公司

NEW WCDP

新世紀・新視野・新文京 ─ 精選教科書・考試用書・專業參考書